This is a wo
incidents a
imagination or a
actual persons, li

ᴐ
ly

First Paperback edition September 2018
First eBook edition Dragons- Rough Draft 2009

Book Cover and Chapter Art by Robert Crescenzio

ISBN: 9781796614992 (paperback)
Second Edition

Acknowledgments

In the course of this book, I have had many family and friends listen for long hours about dragons and this imagined book that I have been working on for years. I thank them for their patience and support.

I would especially like to thank all those friends that did read the unfinished parts and gave me valuable feedback. I would love to list them all, but that would be another book on its own.

Last, I would like the thank all the Everquest friends, who not only read the rough drafts but also let me use their names in the game for some of the characters in the book, especially Shurlok who was a fellow guild leader. Unfortunately, he passed away from cancer. While in treatment he read the rough draft and saw his name and his fellow guildmates as part of the story. He was well respected.

The Platinum Dragon

Book 1 of the Crystal Dragon Trilogy

By Brad Mickelson

The dark shape circled the jagged mountaintop. Rising autumn air, keeping the mammoth creature aloft. Gliding on the heated currents, he slowly closed his great wings, bringing him to rest on the flat outcropping. A couple

3

beats to steady himself, he secured his perch by digging his dagger length talons into the hard surface. Their points exploding small shards of granite off the rocky ledge.

Folding his wings tight to his body, he released his hold on the edge of the platform and crawled to the center of the uneven surface. Closing his eyes, he could feel the elements around him. The cooling wind running over his hard-leathery wings, the hot summers sun beating down on his scaly back, darker than the blackest night. A somber mood filled him as the radiant heat from the jagged rock, reminded him of bad times long past. Shaking his large horned head, he pushed back old memories and tried to focus on the task at hand. The mountain top had almost a meditative quality to it, lulling him into a deeper focus.

Soon he could hear what he had been waiting for, the beat of another set of wings. Dust swirled in the up currents as a golden figure landed next to its dark counterpoint, matching in size and power.

"Thanks for coming, Garath," said the black winged figure.

"Always Dram, but it was a good time for me to get away for a while." Said the other as he stretched out his golden wings, working out the stiff muscle tendons that had held him aloft.

With a toothy smile, Dram said, "Let me guess, does this have to do with a dragoness or two?

Garath replied with a slight laugh. "It would be great if it was only two." Then with more resignation. "I seem to get myself into more trouble than not when I spend too much time at home."

Again, the black dragon laughed in a low growl Dram

4

chided, "Well I wonder why that is?"

Clutching his chest as if he was just shot by an arrow. "You seem to think I did this on purpose, how can you resist the horns on Gardriel, or the tail on Ja'toth, and don't even get me started on that deep blue skin that Sianaria has, it's like the evening sky before it turns to full dark. How can you fight that?" Garath said with a mischievous grin, knowing his argument was lost.

Dram shook his head, "it's not that complicated."

"Easy for you to say, you didn't have to choose. She chose you." Garath instantly regretted his words as a dark, pained look came over Dram. Quickly changing the discussion, Garath asked. "So what mission is the Council sending us on?"

The black dragon inwardly scolded himself for letting such a comment darken him. Garath was not only his closest friend but likely his only friend and was there when Dram met his life mate. Pulling himself together he replied.

"There has been an unusual amount of dragon deaths in the last few years. I have been doing some investigation but can't seem to find a source, or even if there is one. The Council feels with your help, we can finally track down the truth, by moving farther into the human territories."

"It has been a while since we have ventured so far from our home," said Garath.

"Yes, and it may be a while before we see it again. Hopefully, we can find out why these attacks are happening and stop them." Dram turned behind him to see his beloved home, for what could be the last time. He waited in silence while Garath digested what they were about to do. The mission had no easy escape, dragons can only fly about twenty miles before they tire and have to land. In the mountains, that's an easy way out, but on the open planes, a group of riders could run down a dragon just from exhaustion. If they needed to make a fast escape, it would take both of them to fight off a group of soldiers. With some luck, they would find the end of their mission before that became an issue.

"Well let's get started," with that Dram launched off the rocky ledge. Garath, taking one last look at his homeland, followed his friend. Both figures barely skimmed the rocky slope as they gained speed, slowly opening their wings they used the momentum to shoot themselves out over the valley below. From their height, they could make out small streams turning into rivers feeding the thick forests of the mountains. Although not the majestic peaks of their home, the landscape still rose to the sky making the small green valleys in between like emerald jewels waiting to be found among the jagged ranges. Slowly the tall mountains gave way to rolling hills and eventually the flat plains. This was where the humans lived.

The descent to the flowing lowlands was a long flight from the high mountain peaks. With nothing but the wind to hear, the mind tends to think too much. It thinks of things past, of memories long buried, matters that seem all-important to one's self. If not for the mission, what concern could two dragons have for the world?

"Dram, we've got to eat soon, we are getting close to the human villages."

A slight chuckle could be heard from the other dragon.

"Okay Garath, I can never tell if you are thinking with your head or your stomach."

"Is there a difference? Besides, it's been a while since

I've had a nice juicy deer from this low in the mountains."

However, there was a worry in Garath's voice. Dragons had not traveled this far into human territory in years, not since the Greytock Battle. That was a memory that brought too much pain for both of them.

"We'd better make it quick, there's bound to be humans in the woods, even if we are not near any villages. It won't look good if we are rampaging through their forests." The dragons were using their first clear eyelids for flight, although not as clear as normal sight, was not worth risking eye damage. Limited visibility aside, they started searching the woods for any sign of game. Even with their keen sense, there seemed to be little in the way of food. It was as if all the animals were hiding from something or someone, Dram was sure it was not them.

Garath nodded his head. "What's that? It looks like something is moving ahead in the trees."

Dram peered closer at the large clearing. It was part of a dirt road that wound its way through the giant oaks. Flashes of metal were visible in the bright sunlight, meaning only one thing, soldiers. Already they could hear the sound of steel ringing through the woods.

"Let's go in for a closer look but stay out of sight." He said.

Dram didn't know if this was the right time or place to make their presence known. The amount of movement in the forest meant a battle. However, opportunities rarely presented themselves like this, the situation was too good to pass up. Their mission could start sooner than he thought.

Keeping a low altitude, the dragons circled the area. From the ground, they should be hidden by the thick trees that surrounded the clearing. It was a calculated risk, but this entire mission would be the riskiest thing either one of them had done in years.

"Dram look, bandits are attacking that caravan." As they both peered closer, they could make out the difference between the two sides. Well-armored men on horseback seemed to be protecting a coach and four wagons while a far larger force dressed almost in rags were coming out of the woods and pulling the men from their mounts. "This must be a convoy for something important or there wouldn't be this many guards, or this number of bandits attacking them. Want to have a little fun?" Garath groaned at Dram's comment. Lately, his idea of fun usually meant something close to suicide.

"Besides it wouldn't hurt to help someone with a little influence." Garath was a little confused with the last comment. Except for the mission, why would humans be any concern to them?

Uncertain Garath said, "So what side are we on then? The soldiers?"

"Sure, why not, they look like the ones in worse trouble, besides why help a bunch of thieves?" Garath could only give a blank stare at the last comment. Soldiers were a far greater threat to his kind than any thieves.

Dram banked and descended, heading away from the clearing. Garath followed as they reached the height of the treetops then turned toward the battle once more. The faint rustle of leaves was all the noise the pair made as they narrowly skimmed over the upmost branches. The men on the ground had no indication of the danger dropping from the sky. Only Dram knew why they were helping these humans, there was no trust between his kind and any of their race. He could not be sure if this would support his mission or not, but he had to try.

Coming over the last of the trees before the clearing, Dram roared, "Now!" Without needing to coordinate the attack, both dragons knew what to do from years of fighting together. Dram took the left side of the clearing while Garath started to land on the right. The bandits had dragged the last of the mounted soldiers to the ground while one had opened the door to the carriage and was fighting with someone inside.

The sight of two large shapes appearing from the sky, not more than twenty feet away, was more than the bandits could take. Dragon fear ensued like a black fog. Several of the bandits turned to face the new menace but do nothing, too shocked to move. Even using their wings to break their speed, the landing was hard. Fortunately, the ground in the forest was soft as powerful legs dug into the earth, turning their large bodies to engage the enemy between them. Only the bandits still stood as the two dragons engaged, the soldiers appearing to have all been cut down. Slowly the men formed a crude circle as if it would help them against the overwhelming foe. Without hesitation both dragons attacked, bloody talons snaked out claiming victims, nothing the bandits had could even compare to the onslaught released on them. Before the men could even bring down their swords, their life ended, staring in disbelief at the assault before them. Those that were able, ran for the trees, leaving their fallen comrades behind. The fight was over in seconds.

"Garath go after the surviving marauders. We can't have a story of two dragons killing the local populace, no matter if they were thieves or not." Dram surveyed the ground as Garath launched into the air gliding the short distance to the trees following the bandit's path.

On the ground, bodies in silver armor laid among men dressed in ordinary rags. Not one human seemed to be left alive. In the distance, he could hear Garath catching up to the escaping marauders. A couple minutes later, a loud roar and all was quiet.

Now by himself, Dram began searching for any sign of life. If all were dead, he might have jeopardized their mission more than if they had not helped at all. Gently moving the armored bodies, Dram looked for the least amount of life. A crash sounded from his left, he turned just in time to see a young woman fall from the coach. Blood was on the arms of her dress and the long dagger she held in her hand, her hair was a tangle of matted red curls. Even in her exhausted state, Dram could tell that this was not some frail human. Pushing herself up on her hands and knees, she looked up to see her savior. Her strained face was drained of color, eyes wide with disbelief. Just as she tried to speak, the strain disappeared from her face and she collapsed back on the ground. Dram carefully walked over to the collapsed woman and gently turned her over, she was still breathing. Several small cuts covered her arms but no major wounds, she would be all right. Dram thought to himself, this just might be the break they were looking for.

Garath entered the trees where he had seen the bandits escape. The tall hardwoods allowed him ample room as he moved through the underbrush, searching for his prey. His eyes adjusting to the shadows, the dragon could make out several figures up ahead.

Five men turned as the dragon crashed through the bushes into a small clearing. Garath recognized four of them from the battle, the fifth one he could only guess was their leader. He was dressed better than the other men with leather armor that looked well used but still in good shape. The bandits were yelling at the man pointing at Garath. The leader barked some quick commands and the men quieted down and started spreading out to take on the dragon.

Garath laughed to himself at the fruitlessness of their actions. Pouncing to the left, he swiped at the first man with his left claw sending him flying into the two on the right. Not waiting to see the result of his action the dragon lashed out with his other claw at the second man on the left. The blow nearly ripped the man in two as he was flung into the trees.

The leader held back as Garath finished off the last two bandits knocked down by his first attack. Convinced they were no longer a threat, he turned to face the last opponent. The man just stood weaponless before him, unflinching.

The gold dragon lashed out, hoping to end this quickly. To his surprise, the man just ducked under his attack. Frustrated by the nuisance, Garath leaped forward with another massive swipe of his claw. The man simply dodged to the right rolling under the razor-sharp talons. Unbalanced from the sudden move Garath dug into the leaf-covered ground, spinning to face his prey. The sudden move had given the man time to grab a spear from somewhere and now had it leveled at Garath.

The dragon roared in frustration and charged the small pest, ready to counteract any dodge the little man might make and finish this. Too late, he realized the man was not going to jump out of the way, instead had planted the butt of the spear into the tree behind him. Unable to change direction, Garath rolled to his right. In an act of

11

desperation, the dragon reached to claw the man, trying to knock the spear out of the way. The move partially worked as he slashed at the opponent, sending him flying into the tree supporting the spear with a solid thud. Pain exploded in his left arm as the spear snapped in two from the force of the dragon hitting it, leaving the tip lodged in his shoulder. Forgetting the spear Garath searched for any more of the bandits using his inner sight. No life force was present in the area. The leader must have died from the blow into the tree. Satisfied his work was done, the dragon limped back to the clearing.

Dram stopped searching through the bodies as Garath came out from the trees, a large gash from his left arm to his shoulder. Crimson covered his upper body and jaws making his golden skin look like the added color. Violet blood ran from the wound mixing with the red human blood to give a burgundy effect to the color.

"What's the matter, did the little people in rags hurt you?" teased Dram, the wound was not nearly as bad as it looked.

"Do something useful and help me get this thing out."

Dram replied, "Well it's going to suck for flying. Good thing we were walking from here." Garath laughed until he realized how much it hurt doing that.

Dram looked closer at the wound in Garath's shoulder. The spear had been broken off inside the gash, but the head of the spear had barely pushed through the top of the wing membrane where it connected to the shoulder joint. Getting the spear out was not a big deal. The wing would need time to heal making flying difficult for now. The thin membrane that stretched between the bones was the most vulnerable part of a dragon. It also took the longest to heal.

"All right this will hurt a little," said Dram as he felt around in the wound for the broken end of the shaft. Finding it, he pushed it through with one of his talons. Garath stiffened at the sudden pain. The head of the spear was out far enough now that it could be grasped from the top of the wing. Pulling the spear out the way it had gone in would have caused more damage from the barbs than pushing it through. Gently taking hold of the spearhead with his talons, Dram gave a quick tug, pulling it the rest of the way out of the golden skin.

"You shouldn't fly for a while now," Dram smiled, "but I have a plan."

"Oh great, you know how that always reassures me." Garath made an exaggerated display of hating Drams plans but he knew that his friend would gladly go to the Dragon's Graveyard and back if only for the adventure of it. It was half the reason Dram invited him along.

The midday sun shone brightly down on the unprotected meadow. Two large reptiles moved among a field of lifeless human bodies. Neither said a word as they placed the bodies into a massive funeral pier. The last human was laid to rest when Garath turned to Dram for permission to light the pier.

"No. We will wait until the female comes around. The last thing we need is her waking up and thinking we're the ones who wiped out her own people. Go ahead and burn the bandits, be careful of the flames getting out of control. There have been some recent rains, but we don't want to outrun a wildfire."

Garath agreed, but there was still something wrong with this picture. Why were they so concerned about these humans? Why were they even making a funeral pier instead of dining on the tender morsels, and why was he going along with it. In all the time Garath had known Dram there had never been any cause not to trust his judgment. Waiting was not something that either did willingly. Even less when it was such an important situation, but it was this whole mess that made him hold his tongue. Besides, he had always liked a little adventure.

"Now let's take our human forms, she'll be awake soon." As if on cue, a moan could be heard from the carriage.

Dram envisioned the humanoid form he wanted to take. He could feel the magic reform himself, making his body take on a new look. A dragon's magic is part of their being. Not like a human who controls magic as a tool, using words of power channeled through arcane relics and spell components. Dragon magic is internal, like breathing or running. As the more endurance you have the farther you can run, so is the same with magic. Some of the more powerful dragons are constantly using their magic just to try to gain in ability. Dram felt the energy swell up inside him, starting like a warm fire and ending up a raging inferno, beginning at his head and flowing outward. White lights blinded him as he tried to control the power within.

Picturing a man about thirty, shoulder-length black hair, dark looks and a face that revealed no emotion, the dragon formed the energy around him. Then he pictured black leather pants, black over shirt with a leather vest and a raven-colored cloak with a clasp shaped like a dragon's claw. At his left side hung a thin longsword, which by its design was made for use, not for show.

Attached to the scabbard was another sheath with a large dagger, positioned so as he drew his sword with his right hand he could pull out the knife with his left, so as not to have to cross the arms to equip both weapons. As slowly as the light began, it started to shimmer and fade leaving only a dark-haired human, no trace of the enormous dragon that was present before.

Fifty yards away Garath stood in full contradiction to Drams outfit. Blonde locks surrounded a charming smile. A loose white cotton shirt tucked into lightly tanned pants. While he wore no cloak, his sword and scabbard ran from his right shoulder diagonally across his back, making movement through small spaces less difficult. His walk suggested easiness, maybe playfulness like life was a game and he had as much fun winning as losing. Across his chest, he carried a large dagger attached to the scabbard strap. Yet, his most dangerous weapons were the two braces of throwing knives hidden up each of his loose shirtsleeves.

The sun was about to set as they finished their transformations. "We'll need a fire, go get the wood and see if you can find any of the horses. I'll stay here in case she wakes up." As Garath went off in the direction they had last seen the horses, Dram gathered up what he could of the nearby wood and started to make a campfire. The fire was small since they had used one of the wagons and most of the nearby brush to build the pier. Garath would be back with more and hopefully a couple of horses soon.

Thirty minutes later Garath arrived with two horses, one carrying enough firewood for the night. He tied the mounts up near one of the few patches of grass still left after the battle and brought the wood over near the small fire. Turning to Dram, he said. "So, when are you going to tell me what all this mystery is about and why did we try to help those humans?"

"Shush. She's waking up." Dram had placed the woman near the fire covered with one of her blankets. The fall nights were cooling off fast, and her body was flimsy and weak compared to his non-human form. Slowly her eyes opened. Trying to focus, she looked confused, like a night of too much ale and wondering how you got home. Suddenly the realization of what had happened hit her, turning she tried to get up as Dram grabbed her. Panic filled her as she kicked out trying to break the grasp.

"Easy girl, we're not going to hurt you." Garath tried to sound non-threatening, but the strange man's voice caused her to kick again.

"Stop!" The human female halted immediately at the sound of Dram's voice. The dragon slowly let go as the woman turned to face the man behind her. "We're not going to hurt you."

"Who are you, where are my guards?" Her false bravado was betrayed by her shaking shoulders, only by force of will was she able to keep her composure. Dram noticed a small dagger hidden up one of her sleeves. This obviously was not some pretentious noble, this woman had a dangerous edge about her and that could mean trouble.

Dram answered her in a cold even tone. "Who we are isn't important until we know who you are. As for your guards that pile of bodies up there is probably what's left of them." Shock showed in the woman's face, part from Dram's bold speech, mostly from the realization that if any of her men had survived the battle, they would be here beside her. The two dragons watched with interest as the woman thought out her situation, most of her kind would have given up to oblivion with all darkness she had just been through, but Dram still wasn't going to play games with her. She could be helpless now, but she was definitely a person who could keep her head. That was no person to underestimate.

"I want to see them." was all she said as she pushed past Dram and Garath. Her first step was shaky, she would have fallen if Garath had not caught her arm, helping to steady the woman. In a defiant gesture, she tore out of his grasp and continued towards the motionless bodies. Dram lit a torch from the fire and the dragons followed closely behind.

She gasped as she recognized the forms lying in a broken wagon. Under the cart, they had filled with whatever wood and dried brush that Dram and Garath could find. Seven bodies were lying on their backs with their arms crossed over a single sword. The soldiers still wore the armor they died in depicting the cause of death for each. All were killed by either arrow or sword. Dram could see that this registered to the woman.

At the head of the row lay an older man in finer clothes than the rest. He wore a dark burgundy robe with a jeweled belt. Except for the traces of crimson on his lips, he would have looked asleep. The woman walked around the pier and leaned over the old man. She gazed down at the rough-hewed face and gently stroked his hair back. "He's my uncle." She said in a choked whisper. A lone tear worked its way down her cheek then dropping on the cold sleeping face. Another and another fell as she kept stroking the pepper gray hair. Dragons understand life and death more so than most other beings. They know that life is a continuous circle and that one death can feed the life of another. However, massive death for no apparent reason rocks a dragon to the core, for life is very sacred to them, especially their own. Dram felt for the unfortunate alone female.

After a few minutes, she realized that the two men were still waiting behind her. Slowly she took the hand of her uncle and pulled off the signet ring, then placed the hand back over his heart. Turning to the rest of the soldiers, she looked from one to another. "These are, were my guards. Sergeant Ricks, Robert, Michael, poor slow-witted Gustaff too dumb to run from a fight." Her voice went so low that Garath had to strain to hear her. Dram, in a rare moment of compassion, reached out and put his hand on her shoulder. "Sorry about what happened to your men. If we could have been here for the battle, we would have tried to help more. We don't know your burial customs, but we can't leave these bodies lying out to get diseased. We thought this would be the best solution since we don't have time to bury them. We already burned the dead bandits."

"Thank you," Was all she said. Then turning she grabbed the torch from Dram and threw it underneath the wagon into the flammable kindling. Slowly at first, the flamed started to spread, suddenly with a loud whoosh, the fire caught hold as it moved along the dried brush. Small tendrils of flame crackled as they climbed higher into the sky. In no time at all the fire engulfed the bodies of the dead soldiers, burning leather, steel, and flesh. As the woman watched the fire rise, she realized that she was alone for the first time in her life, in a strange part of the country and in the company of two men who she knew nothing about. The terror started to take over her body. The pain of losing her uncle was replaced by the raw fear of panic. Legs giving out, she fell to her knees as darkness clouded her mind, uncertainty consuming of her thoughts. Then as if a torch was lit, the light pushed away the darkness. Years of training cause of her station, helped her keep control of her emotions. Slowly the woman calmed down, but the moment still left her shaking.

Garath held out his hand as he tried to help her to her feet, careful not to scare her anymore. Taking a second to get her bearings she tried to stand, her legs seemed to refuse at first but with sheer will, she forced herself upright. Both dragons moved away to give the lady some breathing room. She turned and looked from Dram to Garath, her heart pounded as she tried to take control of herself and the situation. For the first time in her life, she was unprotected. At no time had she been without someone to look after her. A nanny, guards, and even servants were always nearby. Now she was stranded in the woods with two strangers and a vision of something that she still was not sure was real. Never in her life had she been in more danger, or unsure of herself and her situation.

"Thank you for your kindness, may I ask you to take me back to my carriage?" By the tone in the woman's voice, Garath could sense the panic in her. Dragons can sense fear and uncertainty in other persons or animals. Its part of their survival instincts, when to react or not could mean the difference between life and death. Garath again offered his arm for the woman to take. This time she took it, and without another word, he led her back towards the carriage.

Upon reaching the carriage, the woman turned and looked straight at Garath. Gone was the grieving girl a minute ago. "My life is in your hands. I don't know who you are or how you came to my aid, but my family will pay greatly to have me returned safe and untouched." She said the last with emphasis to leave no doubt in Garath's mind as to what she was referring.

Garath only smiled at the woman in return. Then when she seemed to take it for a sign of aggression, he spoke. "My lady, I doubt if you're as defenseless as you seem, but to remove any reservations from your mind as to our intentions I'll tell you this. If we wanted you, you would be violated and dead right now, not having this discussion with me."

The woman was taken back by his bold talk. No one had ever talked to her like that or laid everything out so clearly for her. Being brought up in wealth had sheltered her from all but the most pleasing of conversation. The words strained her already shaken resolve but again her father's training came to her rescue, steadying her and keeping her mind intact. As Garath spoke, she realized that the danger was not going to come from these two men, but far worse. These two men were all that stood between her and a world that would gladly rape and kill her. In addition to all that, she did not know if these men would even help her at all.

"I'm sorry, thank you for your kindness. Not knowing either of you, I do not know how to treat you. I don't even know your name."

"I am Garath and my friend is Dram. Who might I have the honor of addressing?"

"My name is Danielle. Now if you'll excuse me, I have to be alone for a while." her voice became a whisper as she spoke causing Garath to strain to listen, even with dragon hearing.

"Of course, we'll be over by the fire when you're

ready." Garath made a simple bow, turned and went to look for Dram. The last rays of twilight left as Danielle watched Garath head back into the firelight, white knuckles gripping a brass door handle. She had to force herself to open the door, it seemed her body did not want to respond as it should. Then turning the handle, she stepped into the carriage, stepping into a darkness that was still brighter than the darkness that ran through her mind.

Garath could not help but smile as he walked back towards the fire. For a human, this woman had a strength that was rare in her kind. He had to admire the way she held herself together when her whole world fell apart. Dragons had been driven mad by going through similar circumstances. It would be interesting to see if her strength would last or if it was just the shock of the ordeal.

Dram was adding more wood to the fire. "How's our little princess?" He said in a halfhearted tone. Something in his speech made Garath feel that this was not all that was on Dram's mind. Having been friends for years gave Garath an insight to Dram that few others ever had. He knew when to push Dram for information and when to back off. The time now was for answers.

Dram sensed his friend's uneasiness about the situation and decided it was time to bring him in on the rest. "So, you want to know what's going on." He said it as a statement, not a question.

The two dragons headed to the side of the clearing out of hearing distance from the carriage. Inside the woman had closed the curtains and was rummaging around in the luggage. Total darkness filled the air leaving the campfire the only light for miles.

"This game we seem to be playing isn't just for fun but the actual mission. Sorry I didn't decide to tell you about it before." Garath did not answer but questions burned in his mind, Dram continued. "A season ago the Council came together, the first time since the days following the Greytock Battle. The relationship between humans and us is getting worse. Not only are we held up on our side of the mountains, but they are sending out hunting parties. Three have died in the last year and four more have barely escaped with their lives. Not only that, but rogue dragons are attacking human livestock and some actual humans. This only makes things worse."

"So, what's wrong with that? Things have been that way for a long time." Garath interrupted.

"The problem with that is that is we have a hatching what every ten years? Out of each hatching, we have possibly fifty dragonets? Maybe thirty of them reach maturity? That is three new dragons a year. We lost ten at the Greytock Battle including Andrinin." Dram did not have to remind Garath about his mate. She was knocked out of the air by longbows and killed by foot soldiers before he could save her. Dram went mad, charged a castle as if he was trying to kill himself, only Garath's intervention saved him. Dram did not know if he should thank Garath or curse him. After that day, he changed. In no time, he lost his gold tint to the obsidian he wears today. Garath was the only one that he allowed to be around for any length of time.

"We're losing the war without even fighting a battle. It does not matter how many more humans we kill, they have been killing each other for thousands of years and still they grow. Unless we find a truce, they will commit genocide on our race within a couple hundred years. If we can't find a peaceful alternative, it may be the end of us all." For the first time in twenty years, Garath heard emotion in Drams voice and it chilled him to the soul. For it was fear.

CHAPTER 2

Lo'Lith dove through the sky with mature precision. She was hungry, and the fat calf was going to be hers. Making no sound but for the wind passing her tight pressed body, the dragon opened its massive wings as the ground rushed up at an alarming rate. Straining tendons pulled to bring the wings forward to slow the rapid descent. The calf barely uttered a cry as the massive talon broke the small animal's neck. Without touching the ground, Lo'Lith glided upward, for staying on the ground was not safe for her kind. Not many places anymore were safe for her kind.

Turning, she headed back for the ridgeline where she had first spotted the lone calf. Flying over a small canyon, she strained with the weight of her meal. The warm summer breezes pushed through the valley helping lift her to the heights above. Fortunately, the distance was short for the calf was now getting too heavy to keep holding in her grasp.

Landing on a high ledge, she surveyed the country below for any sign of danger. Satisfied she was alone, the dragon ripped out the soft belly of the calf. Savoring the still warm juices, she could not help but remember the times of carefree abandon. Anything a dragon wanted they took with no fear of retribution. Never worry about where their next meal was coming from. That is all changed now. The humans have banded together. Not that the dragons ever preyed on the humans, but the few that did make them think all the dragons were their enemy.

Starting to feel sleepy after the big meal Lo'Lith curled on the rock ledge. A little nap wouldn't hurt. This was high enough that no man could reach her. "Like the old days, nothing could hurt us."

Pain exploded in her side. Lo'Lith couldn't understand what was happening. How could she be hurt? Angrily she lashed out with all her claws. Something soft gave way with a grunt but the confusion was overwhelming. Another pain exploded in her shoulder, causing her to cry out. A dragon's scream is not something that a man can take without his head feeling like its being torn apart. She could hear shouts to her right but the glare from the afternoon sun blinded her sensitive eyes. Frantically Lo'Lith leaped off the edge. Firm ground gave way to nothing but wind brushing past her soft underside. Finally, the bright starburst in her eyes started to dim giving back her vision. Black shapes were moving toward her fast. Her sight finally clear, she realized it was the rocks and trees below.

Lo'Lith arched her body as the ground raced up to her, bushes grew to trees in the blink of an eye as the ground rushed up to meet her. Frantically she fanned her wings and fought the rushing wind to pull them forward, the air cracked as it snapped tight the leather membrane. Dropping her head, she used all her strength to bring them down, again and again, trying to slow her approach and glide out the landing. Muscles strained while bones felt like they were going to snap. Before Lo'Lith hit the trees, she folded her wings trying to save them from being ripped to shreds by the branches. The leaves gave way as she fell, landing hard on the rocky ground. The force slammed through her knees and shoulders making the forest floor shudder from the impact. A loud pop filled her ears as her left shoulder separated from its socket. Pain exploded through her mind trying to force her out of control. Once before she had lost control and the cost of that was too much.

Turning Lo'Lith roared an angry challenge to the ledge above, half from anger the other from pain. She could see that six men were using ropes to scale down the cliff wall. They would be down in minutes while ten more were running down the path along the ridge trying to cut off her escape. Suddenly the dark veil of fear dosed the smoldering anger inside. In the middle of the second group was a man in blue robes. Lo'Lith recognized him for the ancient enemy. He was Magi.

Forcing down panic, she turned to find any way of escape. Canyon walls loomed five hundred feet on three sides making it an impossible climb with her shoulder. Trees covered the valley floor making flight impossible. Rearing back on her haunches, she reached a full height of twenty feet finding it easier to see past the forest at the south end of the canyon. From her view, she could make out the steep walls declining, leaving a large open plain opening up past the trees, offering the faint hope escape. Once past the foliage, she could get enough of a clearing to take off, leaving her attackers far behind.

Shouts from above reminded her of the men coming down the slope. They had made it halfway down the rock incline and would soon reach the bottom. Turning she limped off toward the south end of the canyon, pain shot through her shoulder as she tried to keep her weight off it. Soon freedom would be hers and then she would make them pay for hurting her, make them pay again.

Lo'Lith used the thicker brush to hide her movement, her green skin helping to camouflage her escape. She didn't care if she left tracks or not, her only chance was to outrun her attackers. Keeping low, she found a dry creek bed that helped hide her large body. Working her way along it, she could see the edge of the forest and the promise of freedom.

Steel flashed in the trees ahead. The other group of men had made it down from the cliff wall and was blocking her escape. Rage filled Lo'Lith's mind as she roared. The ground shook with her might. These weak humans would dare to take on a dragon. Gone now, the pain in her shoulder as madness filled her perception.

Turning she headed back up the creek bed deeper into the woods. There were still six men behind her and being caught in between the two groups was not her best option. The humans that climbed down the cliff should be an easier fight. Not only were they fewer in numbers but the task of climbing down the ropes limited them on the weapons they could carry. Lo'Lith had not seen any shields or spears on them, meaning they should only be equipped with swords and daggers. Weapons a dragon should easily overcome.

The climbers had found the dry creek bed as they followed the dragon's tracks. Lo'Lith could hear them moving down the rock-covered path. Crawling to a position where the creek made a sharp left, she hid in a deep part of the riverbed behind a dense thicket. The foliage and her natural color should keep her hidden until the last second.

The six men were moving fast down the trail. The clear tracks made them overconfident as they chased their prey. The first man rounded the turn in the trail and Lo'Lith pounced, smashing the tiny human into the rocks. Already facing the other five men, she opened her mouth and blasted poisonous gas at her attackers. The green mist instantly took effect on three of the men, gagging and choking as they tried to breathe, their bodies convulsing on the ground. The last two being farther back were able to turn and run. With two large bounds, she slashed at the nearest of her new prey, slamming him into the side of the bank headfirst. Bones cracked as his neck broke from the impact.

The other man had made it into a thicker bunch of trees a short way off, running for his life. Ignoring the pain in her shoulder, she charged after him, not willing to let one of them escape. The man was smart in picking this route since it was hard for the dragon to follow in the dense underbrush, but he underestimated Lo'Lith's determination. Not caring about the pain, she charged straight through taking out any obstacle in her path.

The man stopped as the forest ended before one of the cliffs surrounding the canyon. Turning he found the dragon standing not twenty feet behind him. Lo'Lith just watched as the human stepped back tripping on the rocks. Panic filled him as he tried to crawl back up the slope keeping his eyes at all times on the green dragon.

Lo'Lith slowly walked up to the man, delighting in the fear she created on those that attacked her. As she reached the human, he stopped trying to escape and just leaned his back against the cliff wall. Tears filled his eyes as he tried to catch his breath. The dragon slowly lifted her right claw and placed her first talon on the man's chest.

"Please, Please! I have children!" The man cried hoping beyond hope it would make a difference.

"So did I!" Lo'Lith shouted as she pushed her talon through the man's upper body, skewering him to the cliff face. As his life force drained from his body so did her madness. Having revenge on at least a few of her attackers left her clearer headed.

There were still the men at the end of the woods worse yet, there was the magus. Her best bet was to stay hidden in the woods and take them out as she could in smaller numbers. She was lucky with the six men who scaled down the cliff. She knew that now that the madness was gone, but the fear remained. The foes she now faced had better weapons and possibly armor. Eventually, they would stop waiting and come in force. If they did that, she would make it an act they would regret.

No sooner had she made it back to the creek bed when she heard rustling through the trees. Nine men came out of the bushes fanning out. If she attacked one, the others would move in but none of this was a concern to her. She would make her final stand.

Four men with long spears moved on either side of her as the archers held back ready to fill her full of arrows. Light gleamed off the lances as the warriors set up position ready to strike. As if time slowed, she could see an opening where the soldiers had moved apart leaving only one man in her way to freedom. Without hesitating, Lo'Lith leaped at the man batting aside his sword and slashing him to the ground, her claw ripping through his armor and flesh as easily as air. Talon feet ripped up the earth as the full weight of the dragon launched into the underbrush heading again for the south end of the valley. Arrows flew past her, narrowly missed her large body.

Satisfaction flickered briefly across her face as she neared the edge of the woods. "How dare you attack my kind?" She screamed. Passing the last tree, she launched into the sky, wings beating furiously to gain altitude. Her victory was short lived as pain exploded again, this time in her left leg. Trying to keep herself in flight, she glanced down to see a rope fixed to her rear foot and tethered to a large tree below. She had been snared. Unable to get loose she was forced to land.

Lo'Lith could hear the men running through the forest as she tried to bite at the rope around her leg. The cord was too tough to break even with her sharp fangs. Giving up on her trap, she turned to face the men that started to surround her.

Instinctive madness took over as she surveyed the situation. The four men with spears were the most dangerous of her foes besides the wizard who seemed nowhere about. The archers were nothing but an annoyance unless they got lucky.

Lo'Lith's only line of attack was back along the rope that had her snared, any other direction would be out of reach. Quickly forming her strategy, she acted, launching in between two of the lancers. To take one head on was death for they could plant the butt of the spear in the ground and use her own weight against her, impaling her with her own momentum. Now between their lances, she slashed out sending the men flying into their associates.

The other two lancers did their job as she was attacking their comrades. Air escaped from her lungs as the long spears hit home. Legs no longer controllable, collapsed under the weight dropping Lo'Lith to the ground.

Denial turned to disbelief. How humans could hurt a dragon, something so weak. Blackness came like a storm blotting out the light. Power exploded into her mind as magic long dead kept her from using her own. She could feel large nets cover her body pinning her to the ground. Once more pain came but this time it was too distant to hurt, too removed to feel. Then before darkness took over, she heard the man in blue say "Easy with the prize, boys. We want this one alive."

Then when she could take it no longer, she gave herself up to oblivion.

CHAPTER 3

Garath sat around a small campfire in the middle of the
meadow while shadows danced in lazy patterns as the
flames crackled and popped. Revolving on a crude twig
picket over the fire was a brace of small rabbits, juices

from the meat sizzled as they dripped in the flames. The dragon gazed into the glowing coals mesmerized by the flickering light. He had not said much since his conversation with Dram, but his silence spoke volumes. Everything he held dear in life was just turned upside down, like someone had taken the earth from beneath him and he was falling endlessly, nowhere to fly to, no place to land. Even dragons get tired of flying. The fire spit and popped bringing Garath out of his trance, only lured back by its coaxing twinkling dance.

Dram sat out of his friend's line of sight, waiting for any sign that his friend was ready to talk. He knew what Garath was going through, having gone through it years earlier after the battle of Greytock. The Council knew about Drams ordeal with the loss of his mate and the rescue attempt at the castle. They gave him a reason to want to live even though all they did was turn him into a weapon, a tool for what purpose he did not truly understand. The problem was too serious to let the other dragons know. Rash acts of vengeance would bring the situation to a point that even the great Council could not keep control. That was only part of the problem. To Dram, his friend was a point of light in a world of too much darkness. Garath's footloose lifestyle and lack of responsibility always made Dram feel a little relief from his own inner turmoil. Now he would share that turmoil with Garath, something he had hidden from him for so long.

Garath turned away from the fire to stare directly at Dram, a mischievous grin on his lips. "Looks like we're going to have to have a little more fun then aren't we?" For all the troubles of the world, Garath still did not lose his sense of humor. Then as if a new person took his place, Garath's face dropped, his eyes sagged leaving a face lost of any determination. "What do we do now?"

Dram did not know if he had the answer.

They both turned as the latch from the carriage door unlocked. Opening slowly at first, the door swung open to reveal a boy in his late teens. Red hair tied tightly behind in a ponytail, yellow shirt crossed with a sword belt from shoulder to hip. Blue pantaloons tied with rope at the waist and ankles ran into black riding boots. On top of his head, he wore a red bandanna covering most of his hair. Garath had to smile to himself as he realized what the woman had done. She now looked like a young sailor, which was rare in these parts but not noticeable as a rich woman without her usual protection.

Slowly she stepped off the carriage and walked over to the campfire. Her legs were still shaking but with each step, her stride became more confident more purposeful. Dram and Garath both said nothing, allowing her to sit next to them on the log by the fire. She looked from one dragon to the other. The faces that held her life in their hands were as unknown to her as any she had ever met, leaving no security in the things she was about to face.

"How are you feeling?" Garath asked trying to break the tension that was building for the young woman.

"Fine thanks, just a little weak," she said. "I would like to thank you for your help. Most people around here would not be so kind. I've told you my name is Danielle but in light of our recent predicament, please call me Danny." She then looked up to see if they would offer any comment. A nod of encouragement was all she got so she continued. "My father is a very rich merchant in the capital city. My uncle and I were on our way back from his estates near the mountains when we were attacked. I don't know who you are or your plans but if you help me get home my father will greatly reward you."

Dram looked at Garath and gave him a slight nod. Whatever plan the black dragon was forming definitely involved this woman and possibly her father. Then Dram spoke "we were heading to the sea in the hopes of finding work. Things are rather slow from where we are from, the harvest is done and autumn already setting in."

Without hesitating, she spoke again. "Let me hire you then. I will pay you two years wages to escort me back to the capital. It shouldn't take more than a week of your time." Her voice started to betray a hint of panic as she tried to keep the company of the only protection around.

"You make a very nice offer, don't worry Garath and I will help you get back to your father. What kind of monster would leave a lady all alone out in the wilderness? We should leave at dawn, which should give us a couple of hours to get ready. I will round up any more horses if you two would be so kind as to pack what we will need for the trip. As you probably guessed, we will not be taking the wagons or the carriage so pack light, also we will require money for food and lodging since we were planning on traveling fast and not taking a lot with us."

Danielle nodded and headed back towards the carriage.

Quietly Dram spoke to Garath "She's not telling us everything. I am not sure if it is because she does not trust us or something else, but she is definitely more than some merchant's daughter. Stay here and see what you can find out. I'll see if I can locate a couple more of the horses." Garath nodded as Dram headed out into the woods.

The gray light of morning was taking over the dying

embers and Dram was nowhere in sight. They would need to leave soon, for those bandits might have friends and first light would start searching. Garath wanted to be long gone before they found their way to the battle scene.

Danny had a small pile of clothes and food stacked outside the carriage door. On the other side of a turned over wagon, he could see her trying to free a large chest from under its heavy weight. Try as she could the trunk would not budge causing her to say a few words that although unclear, their meaning was not lost on him. Turning she saw Garath walking over to her, cheeks turned a bright crimson as she realized he had heard all she said. "Sorry, it seems I'm getting into my character." Garath smiled causing the red in her expression to deepen. "It seems like your doing well then, too bad there was no one around to convince. It was such a waste of a good performance." Blush turned to mock outrage as the joke-hit home. Turning she picked up a bag and threw it at Garath. Pain raced across his face as the bag glanced off his injured arm. Danny noticed the look, rose quickly and came to Garath's side.

"Your hurt, aren't you? Let me see."

"No, it's only a scratch."

"Nonsense, those were only clothes in that bag. You acted as if you were shot with an arrow. I have an older brother and father. I learned at an early age that men whine about the little scratches but the big ones they act like self-important martyrs, thinking they will save the world by enduring the pain. Most times it just gets infected and you have to put up with their whining later on." Taking his hand, Danny undid the cuff of his sleeve. Slowly she pushed it up his arm until the whole sleeve bunched around his shoulder. The wound started as a small gash near his elbow, inside his bicep, and then it pierced through to the back of the shoulder. White bone showed on both sides of the puncture. The blood had stopped flowing but the cut was dirty from lack of a bandage.

"I'll need to clean the dirt out. It will start bleeding again but will heal faster." Garath paused for dragon's blood no matter how small, was a powerful weapon in the wrong hands. More importantly, it could be used to take control over him.

"Don't worry I'll be gentle," she said. Garath smiled at Danny's impression that he was hesitating because he was afraid of the pain. Lifting his arm, he offered it to her to clean the wound. The remote chance that someone would find the blood and know what to do with it was negligible compared to the suspicion that might arise if he did not allow her to help.

"Come over to the fire, I have a kettle of water heating up for tea. It will help clean the wound better." Taking his hand, she led him to the small campfire. Grabbing a blanket, she laid it out to take advantage of the fire's warmth. She then motioned for Garath to sit as she put more wood on, increasing the flames to see better.

"I've got to grab the medicine bag." Garath watched the coals light the new wood as Danny left to find one of the soldiers' travel bags. Every soldier carries a bag with herbs, thread, and bandages. The nearest town could be miles away, too far for a bleeding wound to travel. Just having a clean bandage could mean the difference between life and death. Moments later, she came back with a small pouch and small towels. Dipping the cloth in the hot water, she started cleaning the wound. Clotted blood started to flow freely as she wiped the dirt out of the deep gash. Fortunately, the dark morning covered the deep purple of his blood. Garath did not think to change its color on the transformation. Danielle opened the bag she pulled out a small leather pouch.

"This is the medicine kit for the soldiers. Battle wounds are the worst for infection. Something to do with sweat, blood, and dirt, usually cause the wounds to get diseased. The herbs fight the infection, so the wound can heal faster."

Opening the pouch, she pulled out a pinch of the herb and sprinkled it on the wound. Instantly the powder dissolved into the blood forming a thick salve. Garath watched as the salve hardened stopping the bleeding.

"That's the fastest I have ever seen it work but it seems to be doing fine," Danny remarked. Garath, fascinated by the salve, wondered about the strange mixture. Dragons did not have anything like this. Mostly they relied on magic and time to heal their wounds. Something like this would make this process a lot faster, maybe even save the more severely wounded, who do not survive because of blood loss. Danny then bandaged the wound and started to pull down his sleeve when his hand covered hers. She tried to pull away, but he clasped both of them in his lap. Caught by surprise, she turned to look at his face but could only see his green eyes. "I can handle it from here." Starting to feel embarrassed, she tried again to pull her hands away but Garath held firm. Looking down into her eyes "Thank you." was all he said. Drawing back her hands, she stared down at them as if they were burned. "I've got to get the rest of the supplies ready." Garath smiled again as she turned and walked off to the wagon. If she were able to be embarrassed, then maybe she would come out of this with her wits about her. She was a strong woman, he thought, an amazingly strong woman. Grabbing the blood-soaked bandages; Garath tossed them into the fire, where their power would be burned away.

Just then, Dram arrived with two more horses. With the two Garath brought the night before, should be enough to make the trip, using one as a packhorse. Dram was fortunate to find these since most of the horses were killed in the battle. Each soldier carried his own supplies so there are plenty of trail rations, tack, and saddles. The hard part would be taking it all with them. They would have to leave a lot behind and that would include most of the valuables. Right now, the most valuable items would be the ones that kept them alive.

As the sun broke above the mountains to the East, the small party had just finished getting ready for the road. From the south, thunderheads loomed on the horizon promising nasty weather for the days ahead.

Spying the clouds Dram replied. "Could be an early winter this year. I was hoping for better weather for a good month or so."

"Well we can't change the weather, but we can change our position so let's move it," replied Danielle.

Garath could only beam a smile in Dram's direction. "If she only knew," he mouthed. His old friend could only smirk back his reply.

Several hours later, a small group of figures moved along a mud-covered road. The rain had started an hour after they had set out, blotting out the horizon. Water soaked their clothes making skin stick to matted wool. Not much had happened since they had left the battle scene. Danielle knew the way back to her home from the country but that left little comfort for safety on the back trails. Dram and Garath knowing nothing of the area could only offer protection to the young maiden. As modest protection as two dragons could give.

As the day went on, little was spoken by the weary travelers. They were now walking their horses for risk of a misstep. The rain had turned the road to slippery mud and now their travel slowed because of it.

Garath slipped on a hidden rock in the road bringing him to his knees. Pain flashed across his face as the wound on his arm jolted from the impact. Dram, noticing his fatigue, knew that his friend needed to revert to normal form and hunt. Food would be the only thing that would get his energy back.

"Garath, there's a fork in the road ahead. What do you think about scouting ahead and seeing what's up there?" Dram thought this would give his friend the chance to hunt, something denied since well before the battle.

"No!" cried Danny, "He's hurt." turning to Garath she said. "You can barely stand, you would be defenseless."

Garath chuckled. "I'm much stronger than you think. Besides whom would you rather have here for protection, someone with two working hands or me? Without you to protect I can scout without any danger." Danny still did not seem convinced but she said no more as Garath gave Dram the reigns to his horse. "I am much quieter without it. I'll be gone for about an hour, where will you be when I get back?"

Dram looked around then spotted a thicker area of trees ten wingspans off the trail. "There. We will start camp, if no trouble we, can stay here tonight. That will let you recover better. We're not making much progress in this weather."

Garath gave a sarcastic bow to the young woman and walked into the woods adjacent to the trail. Then when he was a couple wingspans in, he paralleled the trail ahead disappearing from Dram and Danny's sight.

The foliage was thick in this part of the forest, the undergrowth keeping his movement to a minimum. Garath worked his way along a small ridge until he could drop out of sight of anyone on the road. A small gully wound its way deeper into the woods and provided enough room for movement in natural form. Feeling he was hidden enough the dragon reverted to his normal body. Although his wing had healed much since the battle, it still was not in any shape to try flying. It would probably just damage it more. He hoped that the water would wash any tracks away as long as he stayed in the gully. Putting his nose to the air, he tried to see what food was near. The rain would make it hard to find game big enough to satisfy his hunger, but small food was better than no food.

Moving slowly down the ravine Garath heard something over the bank. From the sounds of it could be a pig or boar using the rain to dig up the now soft earth for grubs. Slowly Garath worked his way up to the side of the bank, sniffing the air for the direction of his new dinner. Planting his back legs into the bottom of the gully, he leaped forward just enough to raise his head and arms above the bank. Once above the side, the dragon could see his prey. Digging his front claws into the ground, he pulled his body high enough to snag the boar in his mouth. A small squeal was all it made as he pulled it back down into the ravine. Turning Garath used his tail to wipe out the claw marks at the top of the bank. With the rain, it should just look like part of the bank slid away.

41

The boar was bigger than Garath expected which was great since it would sustain him for a week. He slowly ate the rich meal, savoring the dripping flavor. The game was not this juicy high in the mountains. Only down here where dragons rarely hunted was food this good. A strange feeling came over Garath, one of longing for the old days and of power. Quickly he shook it off. The dragons being killed were the ones that could not forget the old days. Humans ruled this country now and as of yet, there was no room for dragons in it. Maybe someday that would change.

Finishing the boar Garath looked around to see if he left any signs of his presence. The rain had started a small stream in the gully washing away most of the mud and his tracks with it. Giving up a small burp from his tasty meal Garath decided to get back to human form before anyone saw him, although no one should be out in this weather.

The small ravine hid most of the light from his transformation as he added a few tricks that he knew to mask his glow. The light finally diminished as Garath realized that the flowing water was a lot higher in his human form than he thought. A waist-high current threatened to sweep him away in the slippery mud. Branches and debris from the rushing water hit him everywhere, finally tripping and pushing him under. Only his uncanny strength kept him alive as the current swept him along, battering him into every solid object that the newly formed river brought with it. Garath thought about reverting to his dragon form but the energy to change form was tenfold that to maintain it. He did not think he could get back to human form again if he did.

Instead of fighting the fast-growing river, Garath started

to go along with it. Swimming in human form was a new experience to him and it was all he could do to stay above water. Foaming mud and newly trapped air made it hard to stay afloat. Ahead the stream turned left giving him a chance to get close to the bank. Kicking with what energy he had left Garath worked his way close enough to the bank to feel the bottom. Instead of trying to grab hold of something that was not there, he jammed his good hand into the mud as an anchor. Even with his more than human strength, it was almost impossible to stay in one spot. His other hand would not take the pressure of the river if he tried to use it. Instead, he pulled up his legs and with his feet dug out some footing in the soft mud. Once his foothold was secure, he released his hand and launched himself in the direction of the bank. Landing back in the water he again jammed his good hand into the mud to keep from being swept away. He was halfway to the shore now from where he started, one more and he would have it. Garath again set his feet but this time the river bottom broke loose denying him the distance he needed. Being so close to the bank Garath finally used his other hand to crawl the rest of the way out of the river. Collapsing on the shore and trying to catch his breath, he realized he would not have much time, or the water would soon reach him again. Working his way through the mud, he slowly moved up to the small ridge that lined the gully. Reaching the top, he turned and looked at the raging river below. To a dragon, it was nothing more than a small creek. To a human, it was death to be in the middle of it. Garath realized that while he was in human form, many things would be dangerous to him that would not be otherwise. He decided to have a talk with Dram about this. They still had a long way to go in these forms and better make plans for incidentals like eating, sleeping, and other things not so pleasant to think about. Catching his breath Garath started to head back to camp.

"Garath has been gone for over two hours, are you sure he's all right?" Danielle commented as she tried to see into the darkening forest. The sun was beginning to set while the dark clouds made night come early.

"We would have heard if he was in trouble," replied Dram. "Let's give him another hour. If he has found something, trying to find him would only alert any danger that he is trying to hide from. If that makes any sense," Danielle did not care for Dram's lack of concern but could not argue the logic.

Danielle went back to finishing their makeshift home for the night. They had brought along one of the big canvass tents from the caravan. Although it took up half the packhorse, now it was the best thing they had against the elements. Dram had found a raised mound under one of the bigger oaks with a nearly horizontal limb about five feet above the ground. Danielle was able to use the limb as a center crossbar for the tent while the raised mound kept water from running inside. After finishing staking down the sides Danielle tied the flaps at the back of the tent to keep the wind from cutting through while leaving the front open to let the smoke out from the fire.

Dram reached for his dagger as a sound from outside the tent alerted them both. A sword was too big for these close quarters. Footsteps were coming closer from behind them. Edging his way to the front of the tent Dram motioned for Danielle to get in the middle close the fire. If someone were to stab through the tent, it would be a lot harder to hit her if she was away from the edge. As quickly as he drew his dagger, he slid it home, "Its Garath."

A few seconds later, a familiar voice at the entrance of the tent asked the come in. Once invited Garath collapsed through the open doorway. Danielle gasped and raced to help him sit up.

"Garath, are you all right?" she said as she helped him to sit up.

"Fine just a little tired, had a little fight with a flash flood." Garath winked at Dram as Danielle looked at Garath's wound. Dram understood the message. Garath was not in any real danger it was just staying in human form that wore him out. Returning to dragon form takes no energy since it is his natural state, but that would have been only as a last resort, and as he could see, there was no need.

It took a bit for Garath to convince Danielle he was all right. She then redid the dressing and used more of the herbs. Again, she was surprised how fast it was healing but not to be aware of anything that could give them away. Garath made sure that the bandages with his blood on it went into the fire. This time almost no blood flowed during the changing.

During the night, the rain stopped and by early morning, most of the water had run off to leave just a damp cold atmosphere. No one said much as they packed the horses and headed again down the muddy road.

A jolt woke Lo'Lith sometime later. Pain filled her as she tried to move but was securely tied down to some kind of cart. They seemed to be moving through an unknown forested area. Her mind was still groggy, but she concentrated on the last thing she could remember about the battle.

"Seems our prize is awake," came a voice from behind her. Strain as she could, the dragon could not move her head enough to see who was speaking behind her. Violently she strained against her bindings, rocking the cart out of control and forcing it to stop. The teamster tried to calm down the panicking horses as they came to a halt.

"We better put it back to sleep until we get to a more secure location." Said another voice.

"Good point, I don't think this wagon will take much more of this." Said the first man as he moved into the limited view of the dragon, his blue robes blowing in the hot autumn breeze. Red hot anger instantly filled Lo'Lith. Forgetting her pain and the ropes she snapped out at the ancient enemy. The effort was useless, the men had done their work well between the muzzle and the securing straps she couldn't move more than a couple inches well alone open her mouth.

As before, the magus spoke a dark spell filled with the stench of the dead, pushing the dragon back to unconsciousness. "This will be a fine specimen for our experiments," was the last she heard.

The rain slowed to a drizzle as three figures passed through the door to the small inn. Heads turned as what little warmth from the fire was cut by the cold wind outside. Quiet discussions resumed as the door closed and

47

they moved to an open table in the corner of the room. The smell of old ale, tobacco and wet wool mixed to give the air a heavy musty smell. Rain showers were the first of the fall in the last week and most had not prepared for them this early in the season. The mood was foul and the tempers short. More than one patron was covered in mud from going about his daily chores. While a few travelers most were at the tavern to relieve the tension after a long, wet day.

Seating themselves at one of the more remote tables, the tallest of the three leaned over and whispered to the little one. "Let Garath or I do the talking, this isn't a good place to test out your new identity." Danielle nodded as Garath waved over a serving girl who introduced herself as Mirriam. After a short list of what was on the menu the group decided, hot stew and bread were brought to the table. Famished, no one spoke the first few minutes of eating, for the last three days had been long and wet. This was the first dry place they had been to since they started this journey. Both dragons used much of their power to keep their human form, not only would they have to eat soon but sleep in human form was only half as useful as dragon form, the same went with food. It had been before their journey that either had fully slept and that they would have to remedy soon.

The noise of the Inn grew as more locals and travelers alike filled the downstairs. "We'd better get a room before they are all filled up." Dram looked around at the rain-soaked crowd. Several were downing tankards of ale and were clearly getting drunk. With the foul mood from the rain added with alcohol, things could get ugly fast. Food was brought as Dram went up to talk to the innkeeper. Purchasing a room might be a little trouble since most poor travelers slept in the commons or out in the stables if the place got too crowded. Only merchants and other rich travelers could afford the expense of a room, but with Danny with them, they could not take the chance of someone figuring out their disguise.

"Innkeeper the smell in here is getting musty from the rain. May I trouble you for a room?" Dram said in a half-carefree tone trying to play the son of a moderate merchant. That would give him the guise to have a little bit of money but not enough for someone to take notice. With the number of travelers in the fall coming back from their summer homes, a spoiled kid and his friends would not be too much notice.

"Five silvers a night and another for damages," said the Innkeeper.

"Five silvers?" said Dram in mock outrage. "Isn't that a bit much?"

"Take it or sleep in the commons, I've too many people and not enough rooms. Now that will be six silvers." With that, the Innkeeper folded his arms across his food-stained chest. This would be the end of the discussion.

"Three silvers and that will include food." The Innkeeper scowled at being interrupted in his business. "You keep a fine establishment here, but that's more than the finest brothel in the capital." Danny then pulled out three royal silvers and set them on the counter. "This should be more than fair for such accommodations as you provide here." The sarcasm was not lost on the Innkeeper; smiling back, he started to reach for the coins. Quickly Danny slapped her hand over the coins. "And that includes freshwater and blankets."

At a nod from the Innkeeper, Danny removed her hands from the coins and they quickly disappeared behind the

49

bar. "Third door at the top of the stairs, I'll send my boy up with fresh water after he's taken care of all the horses."

Danny turned to Dram. "What, trying to give all my money away. It would be different if your father was paying for this trip." Danielle said it loud enough for the Innkeeper to hear and no one else. She then turned and headed back to the table with Dram in tow. Halfway there Danny leaned back to Dram and whispered. "I think I just changed our game plan, let's talk later in the room."

Back at the table, Garath had finished half the stew and all the bread and was now talking to the barmaid. The woman laughed at something the dragon had whispered in her ear. The woman seeing his friends return, hurried off in the other direction, turning bright red.

Danny let out a short laugh at the sight. In all, they had been through Garath had been a small ray of light. Always in a playful mood, he never let the little things get him down. Both sat down and finished what was left. The talk was light but relaxed. With a nod of his head, Dram motioned towards the room. All three rose and move to the stairs. Danny turned and threw a copper on the table. Dinner was usually included with the room, but it always paid to help the serving girl with a little extra.

As they reached the top of the stairs, Dram turned to watch the crowd below. A motley assortment of travelers and farmers littered the floor. The rain and ale left dampness that assaulted the senses. These people were the backbone of this race. A fight broke out as someone grabbed the wrong tankard of ale, yet another pushing match over who is first at the bar. Garath noticed Drams pause and laughed. "You can learn a lot in a place like this," Dram snorted in contempt. His only thought was that these drunk, brawling people were killing his race. Garath could only laugh again as he patted Dram on the shoulder and headed for the room.

The entrance to the chamber was more like a gate to a fence than a door. It looked to have been repaired several times and had a one-inch gap at both the top and bottom. There was no latch but a bar on the inside that swung across the door keeping it almost locked. Little privacy would be granted, but it would keep people from entering. Two straw pallets lined each side of the room with a walkway in between leading to the window. There was no glass in the window for that would have been much too expensive. Simple wooden shutters kept out the wind and rain but like the door, that too had holes and left a fingers width crack down the middle. The howling wind from outside could be heard as the weather tried to force its way in. "Sorry about that Dram, but to pay that much for a room would have caused more suspicion than not. You're not used to bartering, are you?"

"No," Said Dram. "It has been years since we have traveled this far south of our homeland. I honestly didn't know the value of your silver or what the going price was for a room. The last time we stayed at an Inn, I honestly couldn't remember."

"Interesting, I thought everyone knew the value of money around here, especially those without it. What was the name of your people again?"

"Sorry, but we have been away from our people for so long that knowing who they are still wouldn't help you understand us."

"But" was all Danielle could get out as a knock sounded on the so-called door. The boy had finished with the horses and brought water and blankets.

"There's more water in the well outside, and that's it for the blankets. The storm has hit something fierce tonight and we have a lot of wet travelers," said the boy.

"Well if that's the best this place can do then I guess we have to deal with it," Danny replied in an arrogant tone. The boy muttered some sort of an apology while waiting for a gratuity that seemed not to come. After a few seconds, Danielle made an exaggerated sigh and handed the boy a copper. Turning on his heels, the boy could not get out of the room fast enough.

Garath turned a Danny "That was a bit harsh don't you think?"

"I just hope that it was harsh enough. If we want privacy, there is no better way to get it than being an arrogant fluff. There won't be a server around till morning, even then we might have to saddle our own horses." Danny said with a bit of a smile. Since their journey had started, she had been the dependant one now she was closer to her own way of life and was able to help, being more in her element.

Dram made a small laugh at the whole affair, causing Garath to laugh as well. "Well, it seems we are in capable hands after all. Tell me, how did you learn so much about staying at Inns."

"It's the same everywhere, even a home. People will put up with a lot if you pay them. Even degrade themselves if only for the promise of more in the future. If you make out that you are cheap and have a foul mood, then nobody will bother you."

"What about paying them to stay away until you need them, then they would be available to you," Said Garath.

"It would be like putting out rotten meat to keep the flies away, it will just make it worse. Servants lead a very boring life so if something interesting happens they are the fastest to talk about it. However, it works the other way also. If you need to know anything, servants are the ones from whom you can get the latest information. I bet that stable boy is just full of gossip about half the events in his kingdom, and only half of those might have a sliver of truth to it, but that's the way it works."

Dram made a show of being disinterested in the conversation but just the opposite was true. This concerned half his mission, he knew the other half would come in time. Dragons did not understand the ways of humans, that was part of the problem, the other was the most dragons did not care. Dram could learn more tonight than in the last 10 years. His missions into human society dealt more with people who did not ask questions and knew better than to tell of their dealings. If this kept up, he just might pull this whole thing off. Danielle continued to tell Garath about one of the servants back home. One story, in particular, had to do with a serving maid and a caravan guard. Seems that the caravan was ambushed just miles out of town. The interesting part of the story was that the caravan had a secret supply of gold headed north from the capital. No one would have thought to attack such a simple wagon train if the guard had not let it slip about the contents to the serving girl who in turn told her brother. In the end, the guard was dismissed from service for negligence of duty. Danielle was not sure whatever happened to the serving girl or her brother, both seemed to disappear about the same time.

The noise from the crowd down below started to settle down, leaving the soft drum of the storm outside. The light taps of raindrops on the roof lulled the senses putting Danny and Garath immediately to sleep. Dram, on the other hand, had other plans. Not having eaten for five days had run him to the limits of his endurance. Human food was not enough to satisfy a full-grown dragon. Magic can only do so much. It can change size and weight but not metabolism, or feelings or things beyond its direct control. If Dram were to conjure a weapon for him to use and lost it, that weapon would disappear as soon as he forgot about. There were ways around this. If Dram found some steel, he could use magic to form it into a weapon and then it would stay in that form. Right now, the strain of keeping his form and not eating was getting to be too much for him to bear.

Dram walked to the window and opened the shutters. He made no noise that could be heard over the rain and wind. Peering out into the darkness, he could detect no movement. Turning to Garath, he could see that he was awake. Pointing to himself and then to the sky, Dram let him know it was time for him to hunt.

Placing one foot on the window seal, Dram grabbed both sides of the open window frame. Taking a couple practice pulls to see if the wall was strong enough Dram decided he was ready. With a quick pull, he positioned most of his body into the window. Not losing momentum, his feet launched him off the window ledge, catapulting him out into the rain-filled air. With his dragon strength, Dram was able to leap far enough into the night to transform. The distance from the ground to the window was the height of two men. Dram released the magic that held his body in human form. A small whoosh could be heard as his larger dragon form expanded. Black wings swept downward to keep from hitting the ground below, adding a little magic it carried him into the night sky, now he would hunt.

It had been five days since he had been in dragon form. All the senses were fully back, even though weak from hunger and lack of sleep. The exhilaration of being in his natural form was staggering, although now parts of his body were reminding him how hungry he was. Using his night vision, something that was limited in his human form, he viewed the land below. All the colors were different through his inner sight, the trees were yellow, the grass and bushes were green, and the animals were red. The sight only showed living things, whether power or life. With it, his kin could see in the dark long as there was something living to be guided by. The stronger the life force, the brighter the image. Dragons were the brightest of all.

Surveying the ground Dram could see it dotted with life. He could not touch the ground for his tracks would make people aware of his presence, also must eat it completely for no remains could be left for someone to find. Couple small pigs or large turkeys would be perfect.

Banking to his right he spotted an open clearing with several large deer. The animals were too large but at the edge of the field, a group of wolves was crouched. Dram hovered in midair as the pack inched their way towards the larger game. Then the wind changed, the stag in the party raised his head sniffing the air. The wolves, knowing they had been sensed, rushed in. At a cry from the stag, all the deer sprinted for the other side of the clearing, their hunters following closely behind. Sharp teeth bounced off of dirt filled hooves as two of the wolves brought down one of the doe's, while another two took on the stag. The last wolf seeing easy prey started to chase down a small fawn. The baby deer could not have been more than four months old probably born earlier that spring.

The two attackers taking on the stag were no match for the superior animal. From the rear, it had powerful deadly legs and from the front, antlers and more hooves. With each attack, at least one of the wolves took some kind of injury. The predators were trying to keep the stag busy while the others downed the easy prey. Finally, the chance Dram had been waiting for had arrived. The fawn and the single wolf moved more into open ground, enough that Dram could swoop down and grab both.

The gray wolf was right on the fawn's heels. Each time the small deer turned the hunter got a little closer, and then a small yelp as two mighty claws clasped both the prey and its hunter. Dram strained to pull the weight skyward, the last few days was making this a lot harder than it should be. The trees at the end of the field were higher than Dram first thought, he realized that he would not make it over them. Banking right he kept his back arched while still repeating the downward pull of the wings. Finally clearing the small grove Dram spun his entire body into a roll. A smile came over Dram's serpent-like lips as he thought to himself, "this is what it's all about." Of all the things that a dragon could do, he could boil it down into this one moment. The pounding of the heart, taking a flight to the limits, in one moment's time everything was so clear. All his problems just seemed to disappear.

Movements in his right claw brought him out of his introspect. The fawn had died on the ground, the young bones were not hard enough to withstand the sudden jerk, but the wolf was made out a lot stronger stuff. He was just dazed for a moment and now was trying to get free.

Sharp fangs were tearing at the leather-like skin of his claw. Dram inwardly smiled and shoved the whole wolf in his mouth. It was more of a bite then he wanted but after a little chewing, it went down easy enough. After swallowing what was left of the wolf he bit off the upper half of the deer. He rolled it around in his mouth, enjoying the juices dripping down the back of his throat. Finishing that, he savored the last of the fine venison. This was a real treat for a dragon lately, young animals are especially tender, the best were deer and calves.

Feeling the enthusiasm leaving and more of his powers returning Dram headed back to the Inn. The meal would last him for several days, but the other problem was to get rid of the waste. Bones and fur would still come out the same size no matter what his form was. Although he could use magic to destroy the remains, there would be a risk of someone noticing.

There was still two hours until dawn. He decided he had better return, the kitchen would be of making breakfast soon. Banking left, he came full about and headed towards the small town. Approaching the Inn, Dram realized that getting back into his room was going to be a lot more difficult than leaving. It is one thing to release the magic in a second or two, another to control it and change in the same amount of time. Dram hovered several thousand feet above the ground, floating high enough to see the sun start to spread its rays over the sky. It would still be an hour before dawn hit down below. As he scanned the horizon, he could see the dark peaks of home and a feeling of dread overcame him. "If I fail will that still be home, or will there even be a homeland anywhere?"

One last look at the majestic Alps, Dram folded his wings and dropped. The light started to surround his body as the wind rushed by. Dropping faster all he concentrated on was his human form. A thousand feet above the ground the final transformation ended, the amber light faded leaving the human form of Dram falling towards the earth. To anyone on the ground, it would have just looked like a shooting star.

The wind stung his eyes as he tried to make out the Inn. He had now drifted over the barn in his descent. Using the wind, he moved his body back over the open ground between the barn and the Inn. Now the hard part, strong magic gives off some kind of light whether it is yellow, red or blue. The only magic that does not radiate is when you move the basic elements, air, water, earth, and fire. If Dram used magic to stop his fall, a bright green aura would surround his body thus giving himself away, but if he used the wind to slow his fall, it would be unseen to the human eye.

Spreading his arms and legs to give the maximum effect, Dram willed the air to rush up at him. It was similar to riding the high wind currents in the mountains except without wings. The force of air slammed into Dram knocking him aside. Again, he was falling to the ground. Two hundred feet was all that was between him and the dirt below. Now he tried a different strategy. Using the same tactic as before, Dram made four columns of wind race at him and separate just below his body. This left a pocket in the middle theoretically that should keep him stable. If he moved too far out of the pocket the wind would push him back in the same way the first gust knocked him off.

Again, the force of wind hit him. This time, he wasn't knocked aside but was still falling too fast. Fifty feet was all that was between him and the ground. Willing more power, Dram forced the wind to double its force. Thirty feet, 20 feet, 10, Dram released the wind and landed hard the last five feet. Turning around, he tried to see if anyone else was out in the false dawn. Luck was with him, as there seemed to be no one about. Quickly standing he brushed over the indentations left in the mud from his hands and knees. The six-inch deep depressions would have broken a normal man's bones. Fortunately, his inhuman strength protected him. Checking around once more to see if he was alone Dram raced over to the side of the barn. Still, no movement could be heard from the Inn. Sneaking along the back wall of the barn, he then raced to the wall below his room. The window was only 12 feet high, but the old side of the Inn proved more difficult than he had expected to climb. The deteriorated wood and rain made climbing slippery. Working his way up to the window edge, Dram tried to open the right shutter, but it would not budge. Trying again, he realized it was locked. Slipping his dagger out of its sheath, he gently worked it in between the panels. Finding the latch, Dram flicked up with a deft snap of the wrist. The damp wood made no noise is the crossbar swung loosely on the hinge. Holding on with one hand on the ledge, he started to push the shutters open. Suddenly both shutters flew open and the point of a dagger was at his throat. Dram could see green eyes flash in the darkness.

"I would take a kind of personally if you killed my friend there," Garath said with amusement in his voice. Slowly Danielle pulled the dagger away and slipped it back into her sheath.

"You are very lucky Dram," said Danielle.

"I'll remember that," said Dram with a slight grin. Pulling himself up onto the ledge he eased himself onto the floor. Water started to soak the floorboards from the runoff of his clothes.

"You'd better get out of those clothes so that the water doesn't drip to the floor below," said Garath.

Dram pulled off his jacket and shirt, his pants and boots were not as wet since he had just changed form. He laid them out on the pallet of straw to keep them from dripping downstairs.

Danielle is the first to talk. "I heard a noise outside and found the window unlocked. There seemed to be nothing missing but you. I figured I would lock it in case you weren't the one coming back."

"Something was bugging me. I cannot explain it, but it is as we are being watched. I checked it out, but nothing was out there. Ever since we started I have felt as if we were being followed."

Dram was not actually lying. He had a feeling that someone was following them. He could never see who it was, but it was there constantly in the back of his mind.

"I jumped off the barn and it's probably what you heard." Danielle was not completely convinced but could not refute Dram's story. Garath ever the peacekeeper said, "Well since we're all up now, let's get packed and ready to leave."

"Okay, the kitchen should be up and going, I will go get some supplies for the trip," said Danielle.

As the door shut behind Danielle, Dram turned to Garath. A knowing nod was all it took. Both knew that their story was coming apart. They would have to be more careful about what they did from now on. It was getting light outside and the smells from the kitchen below started to fill the small room.

They both had finished packing up when Danielle came back to the room. She held up a small burlap sack full of bread and cheese. Without saying a word, the three-headed downstairs.

The musty smell from the night before still hung in the air, mixed with the aroma from the kitchen. Sleeping bodies covered the floor in the commons. Their clothes were still wet from the previous day, foreboding a cold morning for them.

Passing through the front door, the first rays of the sun were just coming over the mountains, turning the gray into more brilliant colors. Most of the clouds were gone from the day before allowing the fading stars to shine through on the opposite horizon.

They crossed the 50 feet of mud to the barn, while Dram glanced over and noticed indentations from his flight the night before. The only marks that were left had filled up with water, and so had the tracks leading to the inn. Thankfully, the weather would have obscured any signs of what happened.

The stable boy was already up and starting his daily duties. He was startled as he turned to see three figures in the doorway. "Sorry sirs I didn't know you would be leaving so early, I will have your horses ready right away."

"That's okay." Danielle waved off the stable boy. "We have a long way to travel today, so we need to head out. Can you fill a couple sacks of grain for us?" The boy nodded and ran to the back of the barn to get the feed.

Each grabbed a saddle and started to outfit the mounts. After five minutes, all was ready as the boy came back with the sacks of oats. "Good luck to you sirs," the boy said as they walked out of the front of the barn. Danielle nodded at the boy as she threw him a silver piece. Quickly the boy caught it and tucked it away within his shirt. The boy would be quiet about such a large tip. If the innkeeper found out about it, the boy would probably have to give it up.

The sun was just coming over the peaks to the southeast as they started again on the road. The warm feeling on Dram's face and the full belly from last night gave him renewed hope about his mission.

Turning to the others, he said. "Let's go!" All three broke into a gallop heading down the road.

A lone figure watched from behind the barn. He was drenched from being out in the storm all night. A recent gash down his left side of his face looked like a large sword or claw had made it. Sliding back behind the cover of the barn, he headed out into the trees.

CHAPTER 5

"Let's rest here, the horses could use something to drink." Danielle reigned in her mount as the road crossed over a small stream. A crude wooden bridge spanned the six feet of water running underneath. Green grass covered

63

the ground on both sides of the creek, offering some food for their mounts.

Dram and Garath dismounted taking Danielle's horse while she removed the sack of bread and cheese from the saddlebags. The dragons then led the horses over to the grass to feed or drink as they chose.

Danielle sat down on a fallen tree and opened the bag she had procured from the kitchen that morning. Pulling out a loaf of bread, she broke it in two and handed a piece to Dram and Garath as they walked up. Then taking out her knife, she cut several chunks out of the block of cheese and set them on the bag.

"It's not the best but better than dried jerky."

Garath only smiled as he wolfed down his share of the bread and started in on the cheese. Dram nodded as he moved off to the stream, lost in his own thoughts.

"He doesn't say much, does he," Danielle commented at Drams quiet mood.

"He has his times when he gets introspective. It's best to just let him be, he comes out of it sooner or later."

Garath seeing where the conversation was leading decided to change the subject. "So how long do you think we have before we get you home?"

"Anxious to get rid of me already?" She said with a slight grin.

"Well you do kind of cramp my style, you know. I'm sure I would have had a shot at that serving girl if you two had spent a little more time up at the bar." Both of them started to laugh at the absurdity of Garath's statement. The first time Danielle had laughed since the battle.

"Now that the weather is a lot better we should be able to make good time. Maybe by tomorrow afternoon, then you can get paid and be off to your serving girl." She couldn't help but tease him about his last comment.

"Don't get me wrong. A bit of silver in the pocket is always good but we would have helped you at least to get to a town or someplace safe."

Danielle took in the sincerity of Garath's comment, but he could not leave it at that. "Of course, we probably would not have put up with all the whining and complaining we do now." Garath's ever-present grin was smiling at Danielle as he mocked her back.

"Fine then, I will take my bread back and you can eat the dried jerky!" She stated with mock anger as she made a show of putting the food back in the bag.

As if on queue Garath's stomach growled. "Ok, ok guess maybe just not the whining." Again, they both laughed as she handed him another loaf of bread.

Dram tuned out his companions as he moved over to the stream and sat on the cool grass. The water trickled past creating light musical tones as it poured over the rocks in its way, relaxing his mind as the sounds coaxed his attention away from the matters he dwelled on.

It had been years since he was in this part of the country, but Danielle was right. They were roughly a day's ride to the capital. Like a chess master, Dram always planned several moves in advance, while preparing for the worst. This was so unlike anything he was used to. There was no amount of planning that could prepare them for what lay ahead.

He watched as a winged bug struggled for the shore as it floated down the small stream. Hard as it tried to make it to safety, the current kept pushing it back to the middle, forcing it down the stream. Finally, the insect was able to cling to a passing rock and pull itself up on top. Drying off, the bug flapped its small wings and flew off into the woods, disaster avoided.

Dram felt like the little insect. He was in the middle of something that chose his path. Pulling him along to a destination that he did not know. Would he find his rock and make his way back to a path of his choosing or would he drown in the circumstances that pushed him along?

A voice from behind brought him out of his introspection. "Once we fill up with water we can head out." Garath handed two of the canteens to Dram as he filled up a couple himself. The water was a little muddy from the recent rains but still refreshing as they both took long drinks before refilling the containers.

"We will do this" was all Garath said as he patted Dram's shoulder. Like most times his friend's words brought some comfort and lifted his dark mood. Taking a deep breath, he turned and followed his Garath back to where Danielle was making the horses ready for travel.

The cool night air gave some much-needed relief from the day's hot ride. The group made camp next to the road for tomorrow they should be at the capital, being this close to the countryside should be safe. The fire had burned down hours ago as Dram laid on the soft grass, watching the night sky. The forest made little noise as even the wind was calm making and unsettling aura. It was this that kept the dragon awake.

Without knowing why he held one of his swords in a ready grip. Something had been bugging him all night, in fact, he had an uneasy feeling since they left the inn that morning. He just couldn't put his finger on it.

A couple hours later Dram decided he was being foolish and decided he needed to get at least a couple hours sleep when one of the horses snickered. Although not uncommon, it was like a dragon's roar in the still, silent night. Then everything exploded.

Dram was instantly on his feet as two men on horseback raced by him each leading one of their horses. The dragon barely dodged aside before he was almost trampled by his own horse. He couldn't reach the bandit with his horse in between them. Dram didn't have time to use magic, nor would he want the glow to give himself away. Taking a chance, he swatted the horse hard on the front of his rear leg with the flat of his sword as it passed. Hopefully, the horse would think it hit something and panic the already startled animal. It worked, the horse reared up, pulling the reins right out of the bandit's grip. The dragon hurried to grab them before the horse decided to bolt, quickly he calmed the high-spirited animal down. The thieves could be heard racing down the road with their pack horse.

Garath and Danielle were up and confused, they didn't see what had happened until after it was all over. "Dram, the other horses are gone too," said the golden dragon. Dram swore under his breath. "You and Danny go find the other two horses, I am going to see if I can't get our pack horseback." Now that the animal had calmed down, he jumped up on the large mount. Difficult for a normal person since there was no saddle, but his inhuman strength along with his anger nearly launched him over the horse. Getting his bearings, he took off after the two men.

Garath turned to Danielle, "stick with me, there may be more of them out there." Turning, the dragon tripped over the dead fire pit and went sprawling onto the dirt. Trying everything not to burst out laughing she said: "OK Garath, I will protect you if there is."

"Not another word….., they might be listening," Garath said with a slight chuckle, nothing ever seemed to faze him.

They quickly found the horses, they were no farther than the first patch of grass they found.

Dram quickly got used to riding bareback with the help of a little subtle magic. He was fortunate that the pack horse they took was originally one of the wagon teams. It was built more for power than speed and the soldier's horse that the dragon rode was gaining fast. The night was dark, allowing Dram to use his dragon sight while the humans had to trust their horses to follow the road.

The black dragon reached the rider leading the pack horse, still unaware of his presence. Seeing no alternative, he slashed at the back of the horse's legs, hamstringing the animal. The large beast instantly collapsed throwing its unsuspecting rider headfirst into the ground. From the lack of movement, he was sure the rider was dead. Now he could put his full attention to the other bandit without worrying about the first escaping.

He didn't have to chase the lead man, he had already turned and was now charging Dram, sword at the ready. Dram didn't know how to fight on horseback as it was, well alone bareback. He wasn't about to start to learn now, he had the advantage of sight and strength. Pulling up his horse, he held the reins tight keeping the horse still. It was a well-trained battle mount, he could feel it tremble in anticipation, it wanted a piece of this.

The bandit closed in at full speed thinking it had an easy kill, as soon as the thief was close enough Dram crouched on the back of the horse and launched himself into his oncoming opponent. His only concern was the other man's sword, bringing forth his blade he parried knocking it aside as he let the smaller man's momentum crash into his shoulder. The bandit bounced off the dragon as if he hit a castle wall. Dram could hear several cracks from the impact as the thief's chest caved in. Since the dragon wasn't moving, he easily landed on the ground next to the dying man.

Dram wanted information, was this just a couple bandits or someone that's been following them since the Inn. Maybe it was both, he needed to know for sure. Grabbing the man's collar and pulling him closer he shouted. "Why did you attack our camp? Who sent you?" The man could only gurgle a painful response, but his eyes told volumes. They weren't scared, they were angry and filled with hate. Dram couldn't comprehend the meaning of this, but it wasn't the reaction he expected. "Go ahead and die slowly then, your kind deserves no mercy!" he shouted. The man struggled to move as the dragon searched him for any clues of who he was. Nothing, not even a coin on him. His clothes were average for a soldier for hire, maybe one down on his luck. He then searched the other body but again nothing that could tell him any clues about these two. Dram walked back to the dying man, barely able to breathe, his time was short. Still, he had the hateful look in his eyes until they faded away to a blank stare. Dram spit on the body, wanting badly to change to dragon form and burn what was left. "And you endanger my people?" The words echoed back the dragon's own hatred challenging that of the dead man's.

Dram's horse, the well-trained mount it was, stayed near, waiting for what its master wanted to do next.

Feeling he was done here, the dragon mounted and went to retrieve the pack horse. It was almost light, they would need to leave fast before any friends showed up for the bandits.

Arriving back at camp with the packhorse in tow, Garath and Danielle already had the site broke down and the horses ready. While saddling his own horse, Danny noticed something about the pack horse.

"It's lame, must have been from the thieves running it too fast." She felt down the horse's leg as it tried to shy away from her touch. "We will have to leave it here. We have only half a day's ride left so we really don't need any supplies. Let me divide up the food and we can head out."

Dram was somber as they headed out down the road. Danielle was laughing at something Garath said or at him, it was usually the same thing. He couldn't get his mind off the bandit and the look of hatred he had. It was a direct reflection of his own at humans. Did he somehow know he was a dragon or maybe because he killed his friend? The black dragon keeping true to his color, let dark thoughts overtake him as they continued on.

"There," pointed Danielle as they cleared the top of the pass. The road ahead of them traveled down the last of the foothills into a long valley ahead. A large river wound its way from the canyons to the right, through the center of the valley and on to the ocean in the distance. Where the river met the sea, a large city sprawled along both sides of the banks. On the eastern side of the town rose a large keep, dwarfing all the buildings around it.

"That's my home; we should be there by midday," said Danielle, the excitement could be seen in her eyes as she turned from the two dragons and pushed her horse into a gallop.

Dram turned to his friend with a look of his own. More from fear and resignation, it also had the same excitement to it. "So it begins."

"And what fun we are going to have." A smile crossed Garath's lips as he gave a mock salute to Dram and followed Danielle down the red dirt road.

The afternoon sun was waning to the west as they reached the first buildings of the city. The only thing higher than a bush for miles, since the last trees either of them had seen, were back before the pass. Dram noticed that the structures they were passing now were not part of the original city but had grown outside of the boundaries of the walls. In fact, the western side of town had no walls at all. Several bridges crossed back and forth across the river all ending on the eastern side with a large gate that would let them through the city wall. If they closed the gates, the only alternative would be to go back over the bridge.

Dram appreciated the defensibility of the town. With a rocky coast on one side, a deep river on the other, the only angle of attack was from the northeast. The bridges would be a death trap for anyone trying to attack from that side and the rocks would crash any ships trying to land on the beach. Dram looked back up the river and could see no bridges in sight. He did notice a few roped ferry barges that would take over one wagon at a time, but those were very slow. In case of attack, they would cut the ropes to keep invading marauders from using them. Employing the boats in war would be a likely pincushion for the enemy on the opposing banks. Dram could make out the docks running below the southern walls. Trying to land there would also find the attacker easy target for the men along the ramparts. Although it looked like the town had not been in a battle for years, possibly even centuries, it could still be ready at a moments notice to repel an invading force.

As more and more buildings lined the sides of the road, the group had to slow to a walk to keep from running over the throngs of people out doing their business for the day. They were still several blocks away from the city wall and almost at a standstill. Peddlers lined the sides of the streets in small carts selling everything from smoked meats, fabric and even farm implements. Most of the customers were in nothing better than rags, buying just enough to keep them going until the harvest was finished.

As they neared the city wall, the street they were on ran through a large gate, the only gate on this side of the city, from the looks of it. A line had formed from people wanting admittance to the inner city. Three guards waved the people through as they passed some sort of inspection. Danielle spurred her horse up to talk to the better dressed of the three. The guard waved her on as Dram and Garath caught up.

"We don't have to wait in line, come on we are almost there." Danielle motioned for them to follow, as she started to walk her horse through the gate. Dram gave a quick glance at Garath, but he was too busy taking in the surroundings to notice. Dram shrugged it off as apprehension and like Garath continued to take in the sites of the City. Turning back to see the inside of the gate Dram noticed that there were only two guards at the entrance now.

"This way, we should be at my father's home soon," said Danielle. The excitement in her voice was contagious. The last week on the road had been a hard experience for all. Although they had plenty of money, they could not spend much of it without attracting attention. Only the one night did they spend indoors. Even for dragons, it is hard to keep up human form and travel so far on foot. Danielle was not used to such things either, but she held up well with little complaining. It would be nice to get somewhere dry for a change.

The sounds, smells, and sights were night and day to the ones outside the walls. People were much better dressed, the streets cleaner and the buildings were all in good repair. No vendors lined the streets in small carts like outside the walls. Most had shops with creative, colorful signs that not only declared what they were but how they were better than their competition.

The three turned a corner and stopped as five guards on horseback blocked the road. Dram turned to look behind him as three more moved to cut off any escape. The middle of the five guards wore a bright white tunic with a badge of rank on the front, separating him from the others. He walked his horse forward with his right hand up suggesting he just wanted to talk.

"My lady, I apologize for this, but I had to make sure that it was you. Your appearance is rather a new one from when you left. My men and I can escort you the rest of the way." The tone in the guard's voice left little doubt that his offer was more of a demand.

"Captain Norjor, thank you for meeting us. These are friends of mine Garath and Dram." As she nodded at each one in turn. Garath smiled at Dram as he was introduced first. Dram hid his own smile as Garath could always make a joke out of any moment. The two dragons nodded back at the guard as Danielle continued. "They will be guests of my father's, could you please ride ahead and have things readied for them?"

The captain motioned to one of the men beside him. The guard spun his horse around and headed up the street. Even though the streets were not as crowded here, a person could still do no more than a walk their horses without knocking someone over.

Garath started to say something, but Dram with a shake of his head let him know that they should just wait and see. From the start, Dram knew that Danielle was no simple merchant's daughter. If the dragons were just patient all would be laid out for them.

Danielle and the captain moved off down the street catching up on what was going on in the city while the rest of the guards and the dragons followed behind. Occasionally Danielle would look back to reassure them that things were all right. The guards said little during the ride as their attention was specifically on their two new guests.

The small company wound its way through the city streets. The smell of fish mixed with baking bread made Dram's mouth water. Then as they passed an open sewer grate, he would lose his appetite again. Working their way past mobs of people Dram could not understand how the populace could live in such cramped areas. Even the communities that lived near the mountains did not exist like this. He continued to study everything he could as he passed, logging it in his mind for later. No matter how many times he had visited the large cities he always came away with the same questions.

As they neared the keep, the buildings stopped, leaving fifty yards clear up to the castle walls. The ramparts here were not much higher than those of the city although three times the guard towers. Every four feet were arrow slits and the fortifications slanted outward making climbing all but impossible. At the base of the ramparts, a dried-out ditch ran the full length around the keep. Lack of use had let the moat be overgrown with grass and weeds. Water was usually left out of the moat since it eroded the bottom of the walls and caused mold in the lower levels. With the city wall, there would not be much use for the defenses here unless the whole town had fallen already. The keep and its walls were of much older construction than the rest of the city. Dram could make out several areas that had gone through a major renovation, from either war or faulty construction.

A steeply sloped stone bridge ran across the dry moat into the massive entrance to the keep. Any battering ram pushed up to the door would lose most of its momentum before it reached its target. At the top of the incline, two fourteen-foot iron-bound doors opened outward over the bridge. Once closed the doors would have to break in two before they would come inward. If the doors snapped open, it would push all on the bridge off into the moat clearing a way for a charge.

As they passed through the gate, Dram also noticed that the doors were actually huge levers. Past the hinges, two giant beams ran twice the width of the door itself. Heavy ropes, tied to the end of the levers, ran back to pulleys on the wall. A group of men or horses could close the doors with such force that it would crush anything that was unfortunate enough to be caught in between the swinging gates. There would be no jamming the doors open to allow more troops into the inner courtyard. The opposite was true also, depending on what way the door levers were pulled. Very nice design indeed, Dram thought.

One of the guards, noticing Dram's interest, told him that most of the Duke's ancestors were engineers. They designed the fortifications at the keep and many of the city. The guard was about to tell Dram about some of the other designs about the castle when the sergeant, with a polite tone, reminded him about holding his tongue.

As they entered the courtyard, the first trees since they had left the pass welcomed them. Any lumber even near the city must have been used for building or firewood years ago. Only the security inside the keep allowed them to grow for long. In the center of the courtyard, a large marble statue depicting a mounted warrior charging into battle dominated the scene. At the base of the statue was a small pool with what looked like gold colored fish. Dram nodded to get Garath's attention and pointed to the pond. Garath was surprised to see something in nature his own color.

The cart path circled around the pond and back in on itself heading back out the gate. At the top of the loop, a wide set of stairs, almost a wingspans width, rose up to a large set of double doors to the keep itself. As they reached the steps, one of the doors flew open and a host of people came running out. While the party dismounted, one of the more finely dressed of the group ran up to Danielle.

"Lady Lombard it is so great having you back." After his comment, the man moved closer and whispered in her ear. The color drained from her face as she turned to Dram and Garath. "I apologize but I have to attend to something right away. Dribion here will attend to all your needs until I can return. Again, I am sorry." Without another word, Danielle ran up the stairs and through the door.

"Sorry for that sir, we seem to have a small emergency at the moment," said Dribion. "If you will follow me I will show you to your rooms where you can wash up and change."

"That will be fine, Dribion was it?" Asked Dram somewhat perplexed

"Yes, I am the chief steward, second only to the chancellor, the one you saw speaking to Lady Lombard. It will be my duty to welcome you to our city."

"I'm sorry Dribion. It's been a long journey, can you show us to our rooms now?" Things just took a very large turn and Dram was not sure what kind of trouble they were in if any. He always knew that Danielle was more than she appeared but not this much more. The stakes just went up, way up. This just turned into a one-way mission; if it failed, there would be no second chance elsewhere.

"Follow me," said Dribion. Dram did not have to look at Garath to know that he was thinking the same thing he was. Now separated from the only person that knew them in a strange world, they would have to put hope in the fact that they could trust her and those she commanded.

The steward led them to the side of the building and though a smaller set of doors. The smell of the kitchen filled that hall as they entered what the steward called the guest wing. Tapestries of great battles hung between several doors that ran down the hall. One, in particular, depicted a castle being attacked by dragons. In the scene, several dragons lay dead on the ground as the rest were losing the battle. The bile in Dram's throat burned as he stared at the picture. The image was of Greytock.

Although it was not accurate in its facts, something in it hit Dram to the core. It was not that it relayed human's dominance over dragons or that it was the last time he had seen his mate alive. To Dram, it was a picture of the future, of what would come if he failed here. A hand on his shoulder brought him out of his thoughts.

"Wow look at that one, the color is just amazing. It's as if the dragons are right here in the room with you." Garath always one to alleviate a situation played off Dram's surprise as an artist's awe.

Shaken out of his shock, Dram could only answer, "Yes, I have never seen such detail in a tapestry before. Sorry, it's just that I am infatuated with such things."

The Stewart, accustomed to bazaar behavior from those he served decided to explain about the tapestries and the history of the Lombard line. Dram could tell the steward was about as interested in the history as he was. Nothing in his telling was near accurate, especially when he went through the Greytock battle. Dram, back in his own mind, now moved on with the steward as they continued to their room.

"Here are your quarters sirs," said the steward. "Sorry for the inconvenience of having to share your lodgings. Many are in town since the accident."

Dram said, "Sorry, we have been on the road for some time now. What accident?"

"Why Duke Lombard of course, he was severely injured during a hunting accident last week and has been bedridden ever since."

"We are sorry to hear that," replied Garath. "It seems we have come at bad times."

Dram did not believe in coincidence, he made a mental note to investigate further. Not only were two people in the family attacked or injured at almost the same time. Someone else must be thinking the same thing, and that could be trouble. If there were foul play, how easy would it be to place the blame on two strangers that just happen to rescue one of them?

"It seems times, in general, have been bad lately. If you will excuse me, I must see to the other guests. If you need anything there is a small banner on the wall." The steward pointed to a small red flag hanging next to the door. "Just place it on the peg outside the door, a page comes by ever five minutes. They will fetch anything you need. Supper recently finished, but there should still be plenty of hot food in the kitchen if you are hungry. I will be back in the morning to show you to breakfast."

With a slight bow, the steward left the room closing the door behind him. Several lanterns, lit in the room, flickered from the breeze coming through the open window. A small couch and two chairs filled the room with a short table between them. Along the wall, a few more tables with washbasins, writing utensils and portable lanterns for traveling the dark halls of the keep.

Dram walked over to the door to the right and peered through. Two beds and a wardrobe closet were all that filled the small room. After making sure they were alone Dram motioned Garath to have a seat.

"Well, this is a lot better than being on the road now isn't it?" asked Dram, making a show of enjoying their newfound hospitality. The dragon switched to mind speak. *We are not alone.* This type of talking was hard enough in dragon form although essential for in-flight communication. In human form, it was nearly impossible. The concentration needed to keep the form and the fact that magic tends to bounce off itself makes directing thoughts only possible in close, quiet situations.

Taking Dram's lead Garath replied. "This will be the best nights sleep in a month. It seems that our companion was no mere merchant's daughter." Garath figured if they were being watched then not letting on that they did not believe Danielle's story would only benefit them. *Things just get more and more fun, don't you agree?*

"I doubt we will be seeing our host tonight, the steward seemed to believe that we would be contacted in the morning." *I am not sure if you see just how much fun we are in my friend. Accidents seem to be happening a lot around here and guess what two scapegoats just walked into the dragon's breath.* The question was rhetorical. Dram knew that Garath was as quick as any dragon he had ever met. However, he never seemed to take things as seriously as Dram did, one of the reasons they made such a good team. Dram wanted to make sure that Garath realized that the repercussions from this mission were far greater than they first thought. Now the stakes just doubled. If they were found out and it was linked to sneak attacks on a noble family there would be no safe haven for dragons, now or ever.

"Well if that's the case we should try to flag down one of those pages and get some food brought up here. I'm starving." *Don't worry my friend* replied Garath *I realize how deep we are in this. All we can do is be as careful as we can and enjoy our time here. Worrying about it won't make any difference, relaxing a bit and trying to fit in better might.*

It took less force for Dram to laugh at Garath than he thought. "Of course, you are. I would be worried if you weren't." *I'm glad you are here. Somehow, we will do this.*

Giving Dram another one of his mocking court bows Garath headed for the door to put up the flag. Not more than a minute later, there was a knock. Garath opened the door to find a small boy just barely over waist high.

"You wish something sirs?" asked the page.

"Yes, what can we get from the kitchen this time of night? Both of us are starving from being on the road for a week." Garath was trying to make it clear they wanted more than just a light snack.

"There should still be hot roast and bread from dinner. I can run fetch you a platter." At Garath's nod, the boy ran off down the hall before he could say another word.

"Service here seems to be very good." Garath laughed as he watched the boy disappear down the hall. Leaving the door open, Garath sat back down. After days of walking and riding horses, it was nice just to sit back and relax on something soft.

A minute later Garath turned at another knock at the open door. "That was fast...." He stopped as he realized it was not the page returning with his dinner. In the doorway was a young girl dressed nicer than any they had seen yet in the keep. In her hands, she held a folded piece of paper. Dram and Garath rose as she entered the room.

"Sorry to disturb you gentlemen, my lady bids I bring you this and to say she apologizes but an emergency has kept her. She will explain everything in the morning." The young girl handed the paper to Dram and hurried out of the room without waiting for a reply. Shocked at the flyby delivery he was reluctant to open the letter.

At Drams hesitation, Garath grabbed the letter, pausing as he too was worried what it could say. Then ripping the wax seal off the edge, he unfolded it. Unfamiliar words looked back at him. Handing it back to Dram with a sheepish grin Garath said: "Sorry, I can't read that."

Dram looked over the letter as he tried to make sense of the new dialect. Garath never had the discipline to learn to read more than a few languages, although he spoke over ten. Dram was the true scholar when it came to the writings of men. In fact, it was a passion for him. Dragons pass on their basic knowledge in their reproduction. Knowing your history, language, and culture from birth is a great advantage. It has its drawbacks also. Few dragons ever quest to know more of their world. Magic can be used to learn new things like seeing far away places. It cannot make you smarter or be taught a whole language. It would allow you to see people in far off lands and replicate their works. It is up to the dragon to study the language just like any human.

"If I read this right Danielle has had an emergency in her family and will try to meet with us tomorrow to explain everything. It must be the same thing that the rest of the keep is concerned about, the Duke and his accident." Dram was sure he got most of the message. The so-called noble dialect of some countries was almost a separate language, removed from the common tongue. Although Dram knew the common dialect fairly well he still had more to learn about the language in the letter.

Just then, another knock at the door announced the arrival of the food. The page brought the fare to the center table. A small roast, half a chicken and wedge of cheese was surrounded on both sides by a loaf of bread. A second page brought in a jug of some sort of wine and a couple goblets and set them next to the large platter of food. The page that carried the wine hurried off while the first page inquired if there was anything else that the two required.

"Nothing right now, thank you," replied Dram.

"Then I will bid you goodnight sirs. You mentioned you have been on the road for a while if you leave your clothes in this basket over here one of the maids will wash it and have it back before midday tomorrow."

"That brings up a good point" mentioned Garath. "We have been traveling light and only have what we are wearing. Is there a place nearby tomorrow that we can purchase new garments?"

"There are several places in the market you can buy clothes, one of the pages in the morning can show you where to get things tailored to your liking. In the meantime, I can get some clothes you can use until then."

"You have done more than enough, thank you. Tomorrow will be fine. We are not sure how long we will be here," commented Dram. Too much help was not something they wanted to cultivate. Taking a lesson from Danielle, Dram tried not to be too friendly to the boy, or to rely too heavily on him.

Garath reached for a copper to give to the boy as he turned to leave. "Thank you for your generosity sirs but we are not allowed to take such things. It is our lords wish that all guests contribute nothing while they are in his care. He feels it would look bad on him as a host. A kind word to the steward or chancellor would be greatly appreciated. They will see to it that we are rewarded for our duty. G-night sirs." With a slight bow, the page headed out the door looking to see, what other guests needed his attention that night.

"There is not much we can do but eat, get a good night's sleep and see what prevails in the morning." Although

Garath's words were meant to ease the situation, it only compounded Drams uneasiness. Waiting was not one of the dragon's better qualities. It only let him stew over what he had no control of changing. His friend, on the other hand, was fine with his limitations and was more than happy to let Dram do all the worrying.

An hour later found Garath, with a full belly, resting soundly in one of the two beds. Sleeping in human form is something akin to remembering to breathe. Although it takes concentration and energy to keep in disguise, it can be held in control at a subconscious level. Dram, on the other hand, gazed out the still open window to the northeast and his home. The rising moon was nearly full, allowing him to see the outline of jagged mountains. The peaks Dram could see was not his own, more than one hundred miles they had traveled since their journey began, it still touched him the same way. Instead of using one of the down filled beds, Dram fell asleep in an overstuffed chair staring out the window, dreaming of warm wind currents that lifted up outstretched wings, soaring over hidden valleys. To his left Dram saw his mate Andrinin, their wings gently touching in the warm summer breezes. Now they were laying high on a mountain peak. The flat rock heated by the sun warmed their bodies as they curled around one another, sharing their warmth. Now he was above Greytock, fighting the humans that had stolen several of Andrinin's eggs. Soldiers had snuck into Drams layer while he and Andrinin were out enjoying the hot summer day. The eggs they didn't steal were smashed so that none would survive. Ten dragons answered the rage call. They tracked the scent to Greytock castle where the humans were ready for them. Hatred and blind fury engulfed

Dram and his mate, as well as the other dragons. Like the waves upon the rock, the dragons attacked. The humans ready for such an attack, unleashed volley after volley of arrows. Andrinin sensing her last eggs near, dove at the courtyard, the arrows filled the sky and she fell. Dram seeing his mate fall rushed to save her. Even with Dram's speed, he could only watch as the lancers in the courtyard moved in to finish off his mate. Clarity blurred as red took over then black.

Dram woke to see the sun rising over the eastern mountains. Shaking off the dream, he rose out of the chair to face the morning sun. After all these years he thought he would be used to that dream by now, but it still left him drained. One day he would finally live with what happened at Greytock.

CHAPTER 6

The sun had been up for two hours when Garath finally
rolled out of bed. Dram was still at the window half
dosing in and out of sleep. The chair was comfortable
enough, but little would allow him the comfort he

needed. Walking past Dram to the window, he looked out to the mountains to the north. The morning mists still hung in the air between the tall peaks creating islands in the sky.

"Homesick?" Dram asked

"A little more than that I feel so confined, cramped in these small spaces." Dram understood completely what Garath was hinting at. Human form limited most of their powers making everyday tasks that much harder.

A knock at the door stopped their conversation. "Enter." Said Dram, as the serving boy from the night before stuck his head through the door.

Hesitant at first the boy said. "Sirs I have been sent by Lady Lombard to let you know she is still detained. She has provided funds and has instructed me to help you in finding your way around the town and to purchase some personal effects."

Garath was the first to respond. "Is there any other word from Danielle besides that?

Dram was quick to cut in, "Sorry my friend is a little frantic from our recent events. Please give Lady Lombard our regards and that we await her summons when things are more convenient."

A stern glance from Dram was all Garath needed. Without realizing it, Garath had almost spilled how close the small group had become, something that would not have been taken well with the high position that both dragons just found out about. Nothing in the immediate future required any haste. They were in a world unknown to them and patience would take them far here.

"Can you bring us some breakfast? After that, we should be ready to head out into town." The boy nodded and headed back to the kitchen. This would give them a few minutes to talk before the server returned.

We need to take care of our clothing, I am sure the servants expect us to actually have them. Dram motioned to the dirty clothes basket in the corner by the door. If they didn't act like humans, they would surely be found out. They could get away with a lot pretending to be the naive woodsmen but that would only get them so far.

The clothes that both Garath and Dram had been wearing were part of their magic. More illusion than actual fabric, although they could be taken off, if removed to far from either of the dragons they would dissolve into nothing. Leaving people to ask questions they did not want.

Understand, I still have the spare clothes from the soldiers at the battle we can put in the basket while we get new ones.

A new page came back with their breakfast, a hot pitcher of coffee and some kind of sweetbread with honey. Setting them on a side table, he hurried out the door before a word could be said. Both dragons dug into the meal with newfound vigor. They had to do a lot today and they needed all their energy.

Just as they finish all the food there came a knock at the door. "Come in," said Dram, as the door was already opening. The first serving boy walked into the room with a small pouch in his hands. Holding it out he let, the two dragons decide who would take it. "Here is the money for your provisions. Lady Lombard wished that you be comfortable and get anything you need. She also would like to see you later this afternoon."

Dram nodded to the boy and took the pouch from him. He could hear the click of currency inside as he hefted it.

With nothing left to do Dram motioned for the page to

lead the way as he tucked the pouch into his vest. Without waiting the boy led them out of the guest quarters and over to the stables where a carriage was awaiting them. Both dragons hesitated before the door to the carriage, unaccustomed to such a novelty.

"Sirs, if this is not to your liking we can just take the horses." Said the serving boy, mistaking their pause for dislike, something he was used to with guests of the Duke.

"No this is just fine; we are just not accustomed to such treatment," replied Dram as he tried to ease the situation for the young boy.

Looking confused the page opened the door for the two dragons as they climbed in. The carriage had no top, just two benches facing one another. In a small seat to the front sat the driver holding the reins to a single horse.

"Any preference on where you would like to go sirs?" asked the boy, not sure how to treat the guests in his charge.

"Let's start with some clothes, we can move on from there. It would be great to change into something less road traveled," replied Dram.

The boy turned to the driver, "Please take us to tailor Bardow."

With a nod, the driver flicked the reins sending the horse into a walk. Slowly they moved through the gate and out into the city itself.

Barely had the gone a few blocks when the carriage stopped in front of a building with a large sign in front with a tunic on it. No words were on the sign, Dram wondered if that was because few knew how to read. Would someone not do business there if they didn't understand what the words said?

Garath was the first out of the carriage, eager to get on with the ordeal. Neither dragon was sure what was going to happen next.

Before Dram could get out of the coach, an elderly man and what seemed to be an assistant came rushing out of the front door. Eying the crest on the side of the coach the tailor was eager to be of service.

"Gentlemen, gentlemen please come in. I assure you I have the finest clothes in all the capital, in fact, the whole region." Dram was sure this wasn't just a boast, being guests of the duke did have its good points. Only the best was good enough to show his hospitality.

The little man ushered them into his shop, Shelves of clothes and bolts of cloth lined the walls. "So, what brings you to me today? A new outfit for the court, or maybe something to impress a certain young lady?"

Neither of them had any idea what was needed or for how long they would be staying in the capital. Dram decided that maybe a little honesty would help them along.

"Master tailor, to be honest, we are but simple travelers from the north. We helped someone in the court and are now guests of the duke. We find ourselves in a situation where we are not sure what is proper or in style. Would you be willing to suggest what we should need so we don't look even more the country bumpkins that we already seem to be?"

The little tailor nearly beamed with excitement. Normally the people that come to his shop know exactly what they want and how they want it made. This was a rare occasion for someone to ask for his advice. He could actually have some fun with this.

"Well, well gentlemen. I can definitely help you out

then. You will probably need a couple of sets of clothes. Least one for formal occasions and one or two for normal use? I would suggest two, so you have a spare in case one set is being cleaned. If that is alright with you sirs?"

"Sounds perfect," replied Garath. "What do we have to do?"

The little man moved Garath over next to a table with several chalk marks on it. Pulling out a small rope, he asked Garath to hold his arms straight out to the front. Using the cord, the tailor measured him then copied the length on the table with more chalk marks.

After taking several measurements on his upper body, the man reached down with the cord between Garath's legs. Garath jumped back almost falling over the table the tailor was using for the chalk marks. Normally not jumpy by such things, he had not thought to recreate every part of a human body, which he was sure the shopkeeper would find out.

"Hey! What do you think you are doing?" cried Garath, as he tried to recover his balance.

Dram nearly doubled over in laughter. The little man was panicked trying to apologize. "I am terribly sorry sir; I was trying to measure your inseam for the best fit."

"It's ok," comforted Dram. "We have never been fitted for clothes before. Come on Garath let the man do his job." He still couldn't help but grin at his friend, how one moment could make all that they were doing be pushed aside. Garath then let out a deep laugh and apologized to the tailor. He then finished up and asked Dram to come over for the fitting.

After finishing his measurements, the tailor started taking a closer look at Dram's shirt.

"That is a very interesting material; mind if I ask where

it is was made?"

Panic filled Dram as he glanced at Garath. At any turn, they could be found out by something as simple as making their clothes not real enough.

"From the East" replied Garath. "We were there a few summers ago."

"Ah yes the East, they have some very nice materials I hear, but far too expensive for even my customers."

Dram finally remembered to breathe, as the shopkeeper went about double-checking his measurements. Then, once he was satisfied, he turned to Dram. "So, 3 outfits for each of you, am I correct?"

With a nod from Dram, he continued. "And I am guessing you are the more active type than most of my customers?"

Dram didn't realize that might make a difference in clothing but made sense. "Ah yes, we do tend to ride and hunt a lot more than most."

"Great, if you would like to trust my judgment I can have one set of your clothes ready by this afternoon. Although proper they will allow you to move freely just in case your lady friend has shall we say a rival."

Garath moved up and patted the little man on the shoulder as he laughed. "That's always a good thing to have."

The dragons headed back out to the carriage where the driver waited for them. "Seems we got some time to kill, let's get something to eat," suggested Garath, Dram could only chuckle. It wasn't even two hours since their last meal.

After an early lunch, Dram asked the serving boy to

show them around the city. Although the request seemed casual enough, he was looking for something very specific. Following a couple of hours and many questions, Dram found what he was looking for. It was after midday and time to head back to the tailor shop.

With new clothes on, they left the shop as Dram pulled Garath aside. *"I need you to go back to the keep and meet with Danielle. Its time we put a little trust in her, the longer we delay the more we risk. Stay close to her, I think she is in danger. I have something to check out; I will meet back with you in the morning."*

Turning to the serving boy Dram told him he was going on for the night and that Garath would be going back to the keep. "Then you will need this sir to get back into the castle. In case the guards don't recognize you." The boy handed Dram a coin-like piece with the stamp of the duke on it. "Just show this to the guards to get back in."

"Thanks, see you in the morning, I am going out to have some fun." Dram made a show of anticipation of a night of drinking and wenching. Laughing Garath entered the carriage with the serving boy. "Do as you wish, I am going back for a good meal and a decent place to sleep. I have had enough of nights out to last me a while. Let's go." The driver clicked the reins moving the horse and coach down the street. Soon as they were out of sight, Dram turned and headed down a side ally. Pulling up the hooded cloak he purchased at the tailor's shop, he transformed his face, the glowing magic hidden by the thick cloth. Now he looked like a scruffy man, hard on his luck. This was a better disguise for what he had to do next.

Dram found the place he noticed earlier in the day, an old tavern with an unsavory element hanging around the front. Once through the door, he confirmed what he had suspected. This was a place for mercenaries. Soldiers that fought for those who paid the most, not love of country. Hired killers mainly and for that were shunned by most civilized people. Therefore, most congregate together and this was one of those places. Dram entered a world he knew very well, he had been part of it for years trying to find out who was killing his kind. It was most likely hired soldiers, but in all his investigations, he only came up with rumor and conjecture.

Moving to the bar, he ordered ale while he surveyed the room. It was still early but Dram wanted to be there as people came in. Working on his cover story as he waited, deciding that the best scenario would be an out of work merc from up north. Stranded here after caravan duty and too broke to head home. He hoped that it would get him the information on who is hiring now and why.

A couple of short conversations at the bar was uneventful until a tall burly man walked in and sat near Dram at the bar.

"Hi friend, you new around here aren't ya?" he said in a thick accent.

"Ya just got into town, little down on my luck." Dram knew these guys were a tight-knit group but recognized one of their own. It took Dram a few months to get the mannerisms and attitude that would integrate him into their society.

"Let me buy you a beer then, the names Bowlsy, always willing to help a brother in arms." The tall man waved at the bartender to bring two more ales. "So, what is this luck you speak of? You have a strong drink in front of you and good companions, what wrong with that?"

Dram told him his name was Nuis and a story of being a caravan guard to the east, the job ended when the cargo shipped off across the sea. He lost his payment on gambling and women, thinking he would get another job easily. The job never came so he came west to the capital hoping for better prospects.

A few more beers later lead to more than a few war stories between the two, battles protecting precious cargo, women and of course losing money. Dram seemed to hold his own with tails of great deeds enough to convince Bowlsy that he is a seasoned soldier.

"Nuis I think I can help you out. I must go but meet me here in two hours and don't get drunk. I might know someone with work for you."

"I will be here, I need food anyway, and this stuff is going to my head." Alcohol really didn't affect Dram since just like food, his metabolism burned it out of his body too fast, but he did have to make a show. Bowlsy left the tavern while Dram ordered the only food the place provided, a kind of stew. He wasn't sure what the meat was, and he probably didn't want to know. Talking to a few others led to no other information so he waited for the large man to return.

As promised, two hours later, Bowlsy came strolling through the door. "You ready?" With a nod from Dram, he said, "Then let's go." A cheesy grin was on Bowlsy's face, making the dragon wonder about his true intentions. Dram followed the big man out of the tavern and down several streets. Questions were not needed, and work was work to mercs.

Quickly Bowlsy pulled Dram aside into a dark ally. "This is an invitation-only event, but I vouched for you. Don't make me regret it." Dram only nodded at the comment as he followed him down the dark side street. Soon they came to a back door to one of the buildings. Bowlsy walked on in. Dram could only follow having no idea what was ahead.

Through a second door, they preceded, entering into a lighted room filled with men. Dram didn't know any of them except they were all seasoned veterans. Scars on arms and faces denoted battles over the years. Three men sat at the front of the room before a large table while everyone else in the room stood and talked amongst each other. Bowlsy found a spot where they could see the room and waited.

"Not sure what this is about, or I would have given you some warning. These guys want to hire only the best and are going to pay well for it. That's all I know."

One of the men at the front table stood up. "I would call you gentlemen, but we all know better." He said with a slanted smile. Laughs filled the room at the little joke. "You were all invited here because you have some skills that we are willing to pay well for but make no mistake you will have to work for this. We are not guarding something that might never be attacked nor are we fighting something that can't fight back. So, if you are not into a challenge then this isn't for you and there is the door."

After a slight pause, he continued. "There is an enemy out there that threatens us all. An enemy that has killed our people and livestock, one that ceases to hide in the mountains but comes into our lands time and time again to take what is rightfully ours. This enemy is not another country bent on conquering a neighboring kingdom. Nor are these pirating marauders pillaging our more vulnerable points of our country. This enemy is far more dangerous."

Another pause as the men around the room murmured to themselves trying to guess what this menace could be. Dram said nothing as Bowlsy offered up comments about some kind of wild animals.

After the room quieted down, the man continued, "Before I go on, let me tell you that this job pays very well for six months of your lives. Enough for most of you to live out the rest of your days and never work again."

The man paused again to let the crowd ponder on what he was saying. The speaker knew how to get a crowd's interest and he was working them like a puppet master, none of them even had a clue. He paused just long enough to let them think about the money but started again before they considered the details.

"A well-funded group of gentlemen has come together to put a stop to this threat. We have weapons and gold to get the job done, we just need good men. Men, who know not only how to fight, but can hunt, track and move about the mountains. For its not just some wild animals we are taking down." Again, another pause, letting the suspense build for more effect.

Dram felt his dread deepen as the man spoke. There was only one thing that he could be referring to, only one threat.

"Men we are going to hunt dragons." The room erupted in disbelief. Shouts and curses from those that now thought this was all a sham. Dram said nothing just watching the display around him. Bowlsy leaned over to Dram "So think it's true?" Dram's only reply was "do they have enough gold?" He could only think to cast doubt on the validity of the payment at the end of this job.

"Hmm, good point."

"Men, may I have your attention. Attention!" shouted the man at the table. The room finally quieted down.

"Everything I have told you is the truth. We are well funded, and we will be eliminating the dragons for good, providing safety for the entire country. Anyone of you that lasts the six months will receive five hundred gold tremissis." Holding up his hand to quiet the crowd, he waited for them to quit talking. "Plus, for every dragon killed, you will get another hundred for everyone involved."

The crowd erupted in cheers at the mention of so much money for only six months work. The man at the table again let the men get worked up before continuing his speech.

"Some of you may think this is too good to be true, well let me address your concerns. We are going to be bringing a large number of men just like you in for this operation. You are also very dangerous men and not to be crossed, which is why we need you. So, rest assured there is a payment at the end of this for those that make it through."

The last comment was not lost on the people in the room. This was going to be dangerous work and not everyone would finish it out alive. Those that did survive will be set for life if they want.

"Thank you, everyone, for coming. Sleep on it tonight and meet back here at noon tomorrow if you wish the job. This is going to be six months, so I would suggest getting your affairs in order if you have any." No one seemed concerned about the time involved that the man at the table mentioned. Mercs had little ties and six months was nothing for the right job. Most sailors spend years at sea for one contract.

Dram and Bowlsy left the meeting and headed back to the tavern. "So, that the kind of work you were wanting?" he joked as he elbowed Dram in the ribs.

"A little intense isn't it? I mean dragons. That sounds like suicide not employment."

"I couldn't agree with you more Nuis, but I have been stuck in this town for three months. This is the only work that is coming around. You going to do it?"

"I will let you know in the morning, right now I have a lot to think about." The two men came to the front of the tavern where they first met. Bowlsy nodded to the door but Dram waved him off.

"I'm going to go walk a bit and get some sleep. I have a feeling tomorrow is going to be a long day."

Bowlsy laughed and waved Dram goodbye as he walked back into the bar.

The black dragon walked down the street a couple blocks until he could duck into a side ally with no one seeing him. It was past midnight, few were out but for the occasional drunk. He quickly debated about going back to the building and seeing what more he could find out. Realizing that these new mercs were more skilled in the city than he was, he would probably get himself captured or worse, find out what he actually was. Using his cloak to hide his transformation, he retook his normal human form and headed back to the castle making sure no one was following him.

Lo'Lith woke in a square stone room, although large enough for her to move easily it was still a cage. She stayed quietly still as she studied her surroundings, not taking a chance of being put to sleep again. After feeling she was alone, moved to a crouching position, ready to ward off an attack. The dragon was surprised that she no longer had the bindings securing her like before.

Staying motionless, the green dragon pushed out her senses to see what was around. Instantly they bounced off of some barrier on the wall, in fact, all of the walls. Using her inner sight, she could make out the glowing runic symbols coving the oak panels lining the walls. Panic started to rise as she realized the situation she was in. With sheer force of will, she pushed down the despair and concentrated on finding out as much as possible about where she was. Her magic may be blunted but the dragon's other senses were sharp.

Her cage was well built, strong stone walls surrounded her on all sides, including the floor. This was the way the humans built their strongholds, most likely a castle or fortress. Above her was something solid yet magical, never seeing anything like it before, was in no hurry to test it out. On opposite sides of the room were a pair of large double doors, large enough for the dragon to fit through. These were inscribed with different runes, twice as intricate as the panels on the wall. Although she didn't know what they meant, she could feel the ancient dead language channeling the power of the wood.

More minutes passed, and the dragon thought she could hear faint voices coming from beyond the door to her left. So she could not be surprised from behind, she positioned herself at the far wall between them, careful not to touch the runic panels. The human language was faint and at times would go silent altogether. They must be moving as they talked, surmising it was a possible way out.

Lo'Lith tried to concentrate on what she knew so far, even on the best of days she was not the sharpest tooth in the jaw and the sleeping spell hadn't quite worn off. Her life was flying, hunting or mating and on rare occasion fighting. She once thought differently, but those memories were too painful to bring up. Shaking off the distraction she refocused on her current situation. She doubted they would attack again, or they wouldn't have unchained her. She was also sure they had plans for her and must think the dragon was helpless in the magical cage. That gave Lo'Lith an idea, if they didn't want her dead then the runic wood must only be to stop her not hurt her. If that was the case, she should be able to test out her new home a little without worrying about dying.

The green dragon started to study the glowing panels. The symbols and geometric designs were meant to channel the natural energy already present in the wood. That was about all she knew of the subject from her genetic memory. Many things were lost from the old days, that was one of the things her daughter was trying to change. One of those things that got her daughter killed and changed Lo'Lith to the half-mad animal she was today. Once again, she scolded herself for losing focus, none of that would help her now.

Reaching out to touch the nearest panel, she could feel a slight shock as her claw almost touched the wood. She pressed a little harder and the pain increased. Now to test out her theory, Lo'Lith clawed at the panel, before she could even touch it a jolting pain ran back up her arm. As she surmised the panel was channeling her own attack back at her. The more force she used the harder it hit back. Then something occurred to her, taking the back of her claw she pushed against the barrier. There was a tingling sensation but not the pain that her talons produced. She was now sure that the panels weren't the cause of the pain but her own power thrown back at her. There might be a limit, but she wasn't ready to test that now.

She went back to her spot where she could see both doors and crouched on the floor. Whoever set this up was well prepared, this took quite a while to set up. Realizing there was nothing to do but wait, she started to analyze everything since before the attack. Maybe there was something she could use, something to escape.

CHAPTER 7

A couple talked softly as they walked down the garden path. The gentleman, uncomfortable in his new clothes, fidgeted as he tried to make them stay in place. The Lady, although dressed in a casual gown moved with an elegance that made it rival the most expensive from the south of Italy. Her soft sandals made no noise compared to scuffing from the polished boots of her friend. Plants and trees that grew nowhere in the local forest thrived in this sanctuary. Small blooms imported from lands far away filled the air with scents of places only imagined. The couple would stop to admire the rare plants then move on, talking in a light conversation, dwelling on things only important to each other. Finally, they came to sit on an ancient oak bench. Runes carved into the wood were of an old language long dead to the culture of today, but the man with one glimpse recognized the words and the power that they held. The woman motioned for him to sit, when he hesitated, she herself sat first. Feeling awkward Garath sat down next to her as she let him know everything was okay.

Danielle spoke "This was my father's bench and his fathers' before him. No one in my family knows exactly where it came from, only that my ancestor that built this keep brought it here at great cost. When seated whatever is spoken cannot be heard outside this area. In addition, no false testimony can be said while in its vicinity. It is placed at the very center of our castle; some say it is the very heart of it." She paused, and then when Garath said nothing she continued, "You told me that you had something very important to tell me that no one else could hear I figured this was the place."

Garath ran his fingers over the old runes. With his dragon sight, he could see the power pulsate from within the wood. It is normally thought that the runes were the source of power but as a water wheel harnesses the power of the river, the runes channel the woods natural power into something useful. With most animals, their magic is internal, but humans never reached their magic. Instead, they turned to focus on the power of nature to their own means. All through their history, humans have always looked outward, rarely looking inward. Wars and conquest of another land, striking first instead of trying to understand, blaming others for one's own wrongdoings. It is a shame that people with so much potential, handicap themselves by not understanding who they are.

A gentle hand reached up and touched his cheek raising his face to stare at hers. Dark green eyes stared back at his showing him a soul that was kindred to his own. He could swim forever in those eyes, letting their depths surround him, the only tranquility in the madness that encroaches on them both. Gently smiling she said, "There must be something very important to trouble somebody to whom words come so easily."

"Sorry, I seem to get lost when I look into your face." Danielle blushed as she reached out to grab hold of Garath's hand. Fingers intertwining relaxed the tense moment. "But there's something I must tell you, and in telling you I risk everything that could be between us. In addition, I risk the whole reason we came here. I tell you this only because you might be the only one who can help. I can only hope you can understand why I haven't told you before this. That Dram and I are not what we appear."

"You mean that you're a dragon?" Shock filled Garath's face as Danielle made a statement of profound consequences.

"You knew. How? When?"

"Silly Garath, do you think us humans are that slow?" A light laugh escaped her as she delighted in Garath's discomfort. "The last I remember about the attack was two dragons tearing apart those bandits. One was black, the other gold. The next thing I remember I wake up to you and Dram. Your story about coming from the mountains and the fact that you know little of ordinary life, it wasn't too hard to put it together."

"Why didn't you say anything before this, who else knows?"

"No one but me. Back at the battle, I wasn't sure, but I needed help to get back. If you wanted to kill me then you would have done so. When we traveled together, I think I got to know you, maybe even trust you. If not, I never would have let you near my family."

Garath's respect grew daily for this woman, never before had he met someone, human or dragon, that could comprehend so much in life and have the wisdom to use that knowledge. Feelings for this woman were alien to him. Dragons live a solitary life. Once known as friends to the humans, they helped nurture the land and the people, but always they stayed apart, mating only when the urge dictated it. Once in long while two dragons would come together and mate for life. It's one of the most precious rituals of dragon kind. Dram was one of those few and Garath couldn't begin to understand his pain until now.

"Can I now ask you a question?" With a slight nod from Garath, she continued. "Why did you help me back there in the meadow, everything I have heard about your people is that you would have killed everyone?"

Garath had to think fast for an answer, he was willing to share information about himself but not his own kind. There are limits to trust and he would have to decide just what that limit was. "We're here on a mission of peace. Our kind has warred too long, and it was not always so.

We tire of the fighting, the senseless killing. Even if we only tolerate each other for now, it could start a bridge between our people. Someday we may even use that bridge to help both our races."

"There's something else isn't there? Something has happened that brought all this about." Danielle looked at Garath's face for any sign of confirmation. The reaction was not the one she'd expected. As an animal trapped, his face was one of terror. Divided between loyalty and friendship, how could he choose one or the other? He was now standing between worlds. Only the slightest pressure could send him one way or the other. The survival of one people, maybe both, depended on him remaining in that spot.

Dram was right in that they would have to take a chance at some point. Danielle was the best hope they had to build something on. She already knew who they were, now can he tell her about their plight?

"My people are dying as a race." Shock showed on Danielle as the words hit home. Only nodding it was true Garath continued. "Your people are moving into lands where mine have lived for centuries. We have never been at war with each other in an all-out sense, but the constant battles are taking our numbers."

It was Danielle's turn. "Will dragons really stop fighting? All my life I have heard nothing but tales of dragons killing. I know it's true we all kill for different reasons."

Garath looked down at the small hands holding his. They had grown close on their journey. First, he thought it was a playful thing. Both of them seemed to bond together, especially when Dram was in one of his moods, he and Danielle would fill the hours with just nonsense.

Once his wound healed to where he really didn't need attention, their relationship changed from one of being cared for to one of something Garath never really experienced before. This scared him more than the conversation they were having.

"I don't have an honest answer for that, our leadership is more spiritual than like your governments. Dragons are guided more by consensus than any true law or edict. There will be lots to talk about but at least it's a start. If we have a course I believe the rest will follow well enough."

All of this was a lot for Danielle to take in as she too stared down at the hands clasping hers. Hands that she knew weren't real but still, she held on to them afraid to let go. Those hands were a part of something that no logic or explanation could define. She knew deep down that if she let go, it was possible their conversation would stop. That was something she didn't want.

"Tell me of your people." She said as she held his hands closer in her lap. I know nothing of you except what legends have told me, and I am learning that most of those are not true."

Garath was taken back by this; it had never occurred to him that humans really didn't know anything about his race. Nor that they would need to know, for things to progress. It made sense, why have a truce with someone you know nothing about, except killing and fear.

"Hmm, where do I start?" Disclosure was one thing, but what was really important for both races to know?

"What about your religion? Do you have a god that you worship?" Danielle was trying to get anything going with the conversation before it stopped completely. Her own mind was swimming with the enormity of what was just put before her. It was one thing to travel with two dragons that saved your life, another to contemplate a truce between two races that have been battling for thousands of years.

"No, we don't have a god or believe in good or evil as most humans do. We believe more in light and darkness and all the shades of colors in between. The more enlightened you are the lighter the color of the dragon and vice-versa. Not even our own magic can change this." Garath was having a hard time putting their philosophy in words that Danielle could understand. Dragons dealt with things like emotion and feelings more than tangibles of what was an act of good or evil. Killing wasn't a bad thing to a dragon, there was killing for food, for protection, for revenge but there was also killing for sport, for fun or for power which would appall a dragon. Each had a different emotion attached to it depending on experience and values, hate, fear, jealousy, love or selflessness. Right or wrong was all perspective, once a dragon learned this he could see the world for what it really was, from an enlightened state.

"Have you ever done something because it was the right thing to do but it just ate at you inside to have to do it? Doing something that is considered good doesn't always lead to being enlightened. It's hard for me to put into words."

"I think so. You have to understand or believe in what you are doing and not just what is considered good behavior?" Danielle was trying hard to understand but the difference was eluding her.

"That's close but there is a lot more to it. It can also be your view of the world and how you react to it."

"So, I am guessing Dram is the black dragon I saw

when I came out of the carriage?" Garath let out a short laugh at the comment.

"Very observant and yes. Dram has been through some very tough times. Knowing you has given me a small glimpse into what he has gone through."

"Oh really, am I that hard to deal with?" Danielle pretended outrage at Garath's comment.

"No, no just the opposite." Garath hurried to fix what he just said. "Dram lost someone he cared a lot about and more. I won't go into it since it's his story but if something was to happen to you, it would be very unfortunate." Garath smiled as he said the last statement.

"Unfortunate? That's what you would call it?" Again, the mock outrage at Garath's remark.

"Well sure, I imagine that they wouldn't let us reside in such nice accommodations. We would have to look for a new place to stay, I hear the rooms are expensive in town." Both laughed at the absurdity of their ordeal reduced to petty inconvenience. Danielle again tried to keep the conversation going.

"So, there must be a dragon leader or someone the dragons look up to, every culture seems to have them." Danielle tried to change the subject. She had sensed that there was something deeply troubling Garath. As if something warred within him. She also didn't know what to do with what Garath had just said to her. She was just as scared as Garath, only years of court etiquette kept her in check. She still wouldn't let go of his hands but urged him to continue.

"Yes, there is one, Saris. He was the only platinum dragon of our people. He attained a level of enlightenment that no other has been able to achieve. It has been said that he saved our people from a great war,

110

but little is really known of him. He vanished thousands of years ago. Songs are still sung to him asking to lead the fallen to their resting place.

The conversation lasted for hours, neither wanting it to stop. Danielle filled Garath in on the wonders of the humans that although small in comparison were just as matched in meaning. During their talk, both found new insight into the worlds that they now shared. Not only the differences in their races but also the similarities they both valued.

The evening grew late and Garath decided to bring up the other thing he needed to talk to her about, the attack on her family.

"Danielle, I think you are in danger, I am not sure how or why but two attacks on your family at the same time just seems too much of a coincidence."

"I know one of the reasons I brought you here. Don't take this wrong Garath but I must ask this. I told you what this bench could do. Did you have anything to do with the attacks on my family?"

Garath understood her concern. It seemed as if they had known each other for months not a week, it was still a very short amount of time to build any sort of trust. "No, not till we saw the battle in progress then we only tried to help. But your men were too badly injured."

Danielle nodded, pausing to carefully word the next question. "Do you or Dram have any bad intentions or ill will to my country?'

Garath paused also before answering. He was not sure if his dragon powers could override the magic of the chair, though he didn't intend to. The question was complicated, he wanted to answer with what Danielle wanted to hear, but Garath wasn't sure if he could. Again, he had to lay it on the line and see if she was the woman he thought of her.

"I can say Dram and I have no bad intentions toward your country, Ill will I am not sure I can answer that fully. My will would be that men that have slaughtered my kin be put to death. I am sure that you might wish that dragons that have killed humans be the same. But as honestly as I can tell you, I fully believe that a truce is the only way we will survive."

"I know, and I am sorry, that's all I wanted to hear." Neither tried to release the grip on each other's hands as if somehow it was a hope that both clung onto that each was telling the truth.

"The reason I brought you here was that I had to be sure my family and my country depend on it. My father is not well and as much as I want to help you and your people, there are things I have to deal with here. Until I do, it will never allow us to move on."

"You should not be alone though, what if you are attacked here?"

"No, not here, that is why both attacks were so far from home. There are too many loyal to my family in this city, they would never allow what went on. However, I worry about my brother. Jerome stayed up north to take care of business when my father was brought back. He is still in danger.

"This may sound cold but who inherits if your father dies?" There was no easy way to put it for Garath.

A patient look came over Danielle's face as if she had explained this to herself a hundred times. "I know what you are thinking, and you can stop. My father was stepping down, that's why he and my brother were up north. He needed to meet with the different vassals and see how the lands were run. In fact, we started out together, but I decided to stay with my uncle while they moved on to the different territories."

"That's why I worry about my brother. There may be factions that don't want to see the change in leadership or worse could be a coup for power for themselves. I was raised in these politics and even I am baffled about what could be going on."

The night grew late as they decided to part ways. Over Garath's protests, Danielle assured him she was perfectly safe. Arriving back at the room, Dram still had not returned. Ordering more food from the serving boy on duty he ate and turned in looking forward to tomorrow when he would see Danielle again.

Dram got back to the keep a few hours after midnight. The guards let him pass into the guest wing with no problems, being used to the coming and going of visitors at all hours. Quietly sneaking into the room, he set himself down in the chair he slept in the night before so not wake Garath. He finally fell asleep just as the soft glow of dawn lighted the morning sky.

It was several hours past sunrise when a knock at the door woke them both. A court page notified them that they were to get dressed and follow immediately. Quickly putting on their new clothes, they both followed the page through the corridors into the main keep itself returning to the garden from the night before. Danielle sat on the bench with three guards standing in front. Her eyes were red from what seemed like crying.

"Please leave us for a few minutes." She said to the soldiers, but they hesitated to leave her side. "Wait for us at the edge of the garden!" This time her voice left no room for debate as the guards moved off to the other side of the garden.

Looking up at the two dragons "My father is dead, passed away in the night." Garath pushing aside etiquette sat down next to her. Losing her composer, she buried her face into Garath's chest as he put his arm around her for comfort. Tears flowed again as she could no longer hold them back.

"I don't understand, he was getting better, then just gone." Both dragons could say nothing as she softly cried, knowing that, just them being here, was some form of comfort. Letting her mourn her kin, something she had not done since they met.

"I'm sorry I know this is not your concern."

"You are our concern, and so is this. We are sorry for your loss." Garath tried to console her but there was little if anything he could say that would do any good.

Lifting her head, she looked up into the green eyes that seemed to comfort her without knowing why. Eyes that were as alien to everything she ever knew, that she trusted would never let her down.

Pulling herself together, she turned to Dram, "We need to talk."

"Yes, we do. Far more has happened since yesterday than you know." Garath told Dram of the bench and the power it held. Sitting down he told them of the meeting he went to the night before as his friend caught him up on what he told Danielle and their conversation the previous evening. Things had changed for the worse, much worse.

"Then we are in more trouble than either of us had known." Danielle continued "something I didn't tell Garath because I wanted to talk to my father first."

114

Taking a deep breath, she went on "I am told he was hunting a dragon when he was injured, and now quite a few people know of it. I'm sorry but any talks of peace right now I'm afraid won't do anything but cause dissension. From what you said about the mercenaries, people are already taking things into their own hands."

Dram only nodded. True or not, the story would spread. Any chance of finding some common ground was nearly impossible now.

"I am having horses ready to travel to my brother. He is now the ruler of our country, but more I am sure he is in danger. You two are welcome to come with me. There may be some hope if I can talk to him about your proposal."

Dram went over the situation in his mind. Something was definitely not right beyond the circumstances that were occurring. Too much was happening at the same time to be a coincidence. She was right though; her brother was in danger. They all were until they could find out who was behind all this.

"Garath, you will go with Danielle. Stay close to her, I am going back to see who is behind the hiring of the mercenaries. It might be better if only one of us is there to talk to your brother. Both of us might not look as peaceful as we intend."

Danielle started to object but Dram cut her off. "Garath can protect you better than anyone. If there is nothing amiss, we don't lose a thing. If someone is planning to get your family out of the way, I can't think of anyone better." Finally agreeing with Dram, they made plans for a cover story for Garath. The human form would not be the best way to approach the new ruler. He would travel with Danielle's group part way and leave the group. Then in his true form follow them, hopefully with her help would be able to talk to her brother about their mission with no deception.

Danielle called the guards back over as the two dragons left to head back to their room. Dram grabbed the worst of the clothing left over from the guards. He would need to look the part and nice clothing wouldn't do it. Leaving Garath the rest of what the tailor had made for them, he turned to his old friend.

"I know I can count on you but be careful. I have a very bad feeling about this."

Garath smiled at his friend's concern. "You are going to infiltrate a group of dragon slayers and you are worried about me? I will be fine, and when we get to her brother I will try to get this truce going."

A knowing look was all Dram could do as he hefted his pack and left the room. What Garath had said hit him more than he dared to admit. He was doing the most dangerous thing he could imagine. Not just life or death but he had to find out who was behind this new order and stop them, one way or another.

Dram turned back to see his friend once more. "Good luck Dram." Nodding all he could say was "you too." Turning he walked out of their room and down the hall.

Lo'Lith quickly woke to the sound of several men outside the door where she had heard the voices before. This time it sounded like someone was working the lock, soon there was a final click and the doors started to swing inward. The dragon was ready to spring at any opportunity. She had already gone over this a hundred times in her mind, surprise and speed would be her strength. Battling them would only allow time for more soldiers to come, she would get past the soldiers and head for any opening to the outside she could find.

Now the double doors were fully opened, several men were coming into the room including the magi. Bile rose in the dragon's throat at the site, it was now or never, the men were only ten feet away. Springing forward, Lo'Lith pounced straight at the mage, maybe she could disrupt his spellcasting long enough to get past. Five feet, then two, it was going to work. Suddenly pain exploded across her face and shoulder as she hit an invisible barrier, starbursts filled the air not only from the magical wall but her own head hitting the immovable object.

The men in the room laughed as the wizard sneered, "You dragons are all so foolish and predictable, you would think one of you would do something different."

Dread filled Lo'Lith as she realized she was not the first dragon to be caged here, worse where were they now? Was that to be her fate? Enough she thought, this ends now. Inhaling to use her breath weapon, there was another comment from the mage. "I wouldn't do that if I were you." The dragon paused, "you think we didn't account for that? Your poison won't cross the barrier but will surround you instead. I imagine your skin can take it but what about your eyes? I imagine you have other sensitive parts?"

The green dragon halted, not knowing what to do. She was pretty sure the magus was correct from what she had seen so far in the cage. Still, she could not give in, bringing her magic to bare she shot an energy bolt at the wizard. It ricocheted off the invisible wall and bounced around the room nearly hitting Lo'Lith.

"Nice," said the wizard, "but we don't want you to

injure yourself. We want to do that." He now spoke another spell and a force came crushing down on the dragon. Try as she could the force pinned her to the floor, unable to move.

From her position, Lo'Lith could only see the men from her right eye. The wizard nodded to one of the soldiers while pulling out a small hatchet from his robes, he handed it over to the reluctant attacker. "Don't worry, it can't do anything right now. Bring me one of its talons on the right foot." Without hesitation, the man walked through the barrier, kneeled down he chopped the blade cleanly through the foot-long appendage at the start of the claw.

Lo'Lith screamed in pain and anger, finding power from somewhere she slowly started to rise, fighting the powerful magic holding her down. Surprised the mage quickly enchanted another spell slamming the dragon back to the ground. "Seems we have a fighter here, good. That will help test the latest batch even better. I have to hold it down while you do the testing, I would put it back to sleep but that will ruin the test results."

A better-dressed man next to the wizard nodded and said. "I will bring in the cart, just make sure you keep a tight leash on that thing. That first dragon we captured almost took my head off."

"Good thing you are well trained, My Lord." The mage said with a wicked smile. The other man grunted at the useless argument and walked out the double doors. Quickly he returned with a rolling cart filled with vials of a green liquid and a stack of dagger length needles. He unstoppered a flask and dipped one of the sharp metal rods into the mixture.

"OK, hold it tight!" Said the lord as the magi focused on

118

keeping the creature restrained. With skilled precision, he slowly pushed the rod into Lo'Lith's claw where they removed the talon. The dragon screamed from the pain, burning like the fire from a thousand dragons, unimaginably worse than the cutting. While she still screamed, the man walked back and picked up an empty bottle and returned to the claw with the metal rod in it.

"It's still not right. Close, but we are going to need a few more tests. Let me get some blood to analyze." The man put the mouth of the empty flask up to the still open wound. Putting his boot on the claw he gave a hard stomp shooting dragon blood out of the claw and into the bottle. Lo'Lith's screams continued.

"I am going to test a couple more spots for dermal reaction, we are really close I can feel it." The man walked back to the magi who was now holding the severed talon. "Concentrate, you can play with your toys later." The mage's smile mirrored that of the man as he grabbed a few more needles and coated them with the liquid.

The test was over quickly but the dragon's screams went long into the night.

CHAPTER 8

Dram turned down the street from the night before.
Several men were already gathered in the small ally with
their packs and gear. Bowlsy was there, leaning up

against the building with a large round shield at his feet. Noticing Dram, he waved him over.

"They are having us wait out here, seems there is going to be a lot of people."

Dram dropped his gear off in the shade of the building next to his new friend. The day was starting to get hot, probably one of the last before winter started to set in. It was late autumn already, with maybe only a couple weeks until the bad weather hit. Noticing the shield at Bowlsy's feet, he took a close look at the faded picture on it. Although scratched up, it was well-made and solid steel, a very expensive item for a merc to have.

"That's a crest isn't it?" Dram was familiar with the heraldry of the area, but this one he didn't recognize. Even the style was alien to the local nobility.

Bowlsy smiled, a habit that he seemed to do when he was about to tell a story. That was usually all the time. "Well see I was traveling with this caravan heading through some really bad bandit country. The owner of the caravan was a minor noble of some rank that meant he was barely above us common folks. Well, we got attacked right before dawn one morning; there we were four of us against fifteen bandits. The noble had some fancy armor but didn't know which hand to put the shield in and which the sword. Anyways my shield broke in two from a huge battleaxe their leader wielded. So, I grabbed the shield out of his hand and proceeded to beat back the bandits with the help of the other two guards. The noble let me keep the shield for saving his life; this thing has gotten me out of a lot of scrapes."

It was a bit past noon when three wagons rolled up in front of the alley. As they stopped one of the men from the night before came out of the door they used to get into the meeting hall.

"Men grab your gear and load up, there is a lot of you so try and make do, we only have an hour of travel to get to the meeting area."

Twenty-five men give or take loaded into the wagons. While space was tight, it was not uncomfortable. As soon as everyone was loaded, the wagons moved out of the city. Most everyone was in good spirits at the prospect of finally getting work. Talks of battles and women filled their time as they moved northwest of the city across the river. An hour later brought them to a staging ground. Two large tents sat next to an open dirt area surrounded by more of the same kind of wagons that were bringing their group in. Worse was the number of men standing around the tents, with the number of wagons parked there it must be almost two hundred men. Gathered, he conjectured, from all over the country. This was very bad news.

"Unload and meet over by the tents, you are the last ones to arrive, so we can get started." As all the mercs assembled, the three men from the night before were once again at a table set up between the tents.

"We have had a lot more turn out than we expected. We are going to pair people off and test their skills. Those not accepted will be given five silvers for your time and transport home."

"Wonder who I am going to be able to beat up?" Bowlsy told Dram louder than he wanted.

The man at the table was not happy being interrupted in his speech. Pointing at the both of them, he said "You two, why don't you lead us off."

Bowlsy didn't hesitate as he backhanded his large shield into Dram's chest knocking him to the ground. Rolling over his back from the blow, he drew his swords barely in time to block a nasty overhead slash from Bowlsy's weapon. Regaining his focus, he slashed out with his right sword, feigning at his opponents shield while coming in with the left to try to work inside the large man's defenses. Bowlsy was ready for him, catching one weapon on the shield he flipped his sword inside and deflected Dram's other attack. Without hesitating, Bowlsy slid his shield down his opponent's blade ramming it into his chest. Again, Dram went flying backwards. The dragon had never seen someone use a shield as a weapon. Knowing an attack could come from any side he changed tactics, approaching light and fast he tried to dodge the attacks from both sword and shield while getting inside his defenses. Each opponent parried, ducked, blocked to a standstill. Dram, thinking he finally had him, moved in. Bowlsy didn't block the attack but lifted his shield so that Dram followed through and became overextended. Bowlsy clamped down on his right hand pinning it between the shield and his body. Flipping his sword again, he blocked Dram's other blade and delivered a right-handed punch to his jaw.

"That's enough you both made it, come up to the table and get a red armband. You two, show me what you got." Two other mercs started to fight, trying to gain the position.

Bowlsy still held Dram's arm, now to hold him up more than battle him. "Walk it off, I didn't hit you that hard."

"Hard enough I am still seeing stars, what the hell was all that about?" Bowlsy released his arm as Dram tried to steady himself. Bowlsy just smiled as he grabbed Dram's shoulder and pushed him over to the table to get an armband. "I smell food, now that we have the job I'm sure that is for us. Hopefully, they have some ale also; I got thirsty knocking you on the ground."

Dram could only laugh as he followed the big man into one of the tents. Food had been set up for the men along with a couple casks of ale. Seems their employers wanted to keep them in good spirits. Each grabbing a plate of food and a mug of ale they headed back out of the tent to sit at one of the tables lining the side. More men were being processed and not all were making the cut. They didn't say how many men they were going to hire but by the number of red bands in the box, he guessed over one hundred.

"So, you are not used to fighting larger opponents, are you?" Bowlsy teased him, referring to his fighting skills today.

"No, most of my opponents are smaller than me." Dram smiled to himself, in dragon form, all his opponents were smaller than he was. Even in human form, he was still a couple inches taller than most men. Bowlsy, on the other hand, was four inches taller and probably outweighed him by fifty pounds or more. Despite his size though, Bowlsy moved as quick as anyone he had ever seen. Dram wasn't a master swordsman by any means, but he could hold his own. The reason he chose two swords was that it was close to how he fought in dragon form.

"You come in from the top and sides a lot in your attacks, for most of your opponents that probably works just fine. But with guys like me, unless you get a lucky shot you won't have the leverage to do any damage even if you do get past my defenses. If you stay low on your attacks even the biggest guy or animal will go down if they can't stand."

What Bowlsy said made sense, take out a knee or leg and even the biggest opponent would drop like a rock. Without being able to get over the top of someone, it was hard to put the power behind your stroke to cut through armor. So even getting past the shield it would do little damage.

"I doubt we are going anywhere for the rest of the day, there still is a lot of people that need to be weeded out. How about I show you a few moves?"

They practiced for a few hours as the last of the mercs were separated into two groups. Those that didn't make the cut were given their silver and carted away back home. It was still three hours or so before sunset when those remaining were again gathered up for an announcement.

"Men we have a week's journey ahead of us, we leave in the morning at first light. I suggest you be ready, but in the meantime, there is food and ale. Enjoy yourselves."

Dram counted over one hundred men in the camp. He still had no idea of who was behind all this or what plans they had for everyone.

Dram circled his larger opponent, waiting for an opening to strike. With each feint of his sword, the man before him countered showing no weakness to be taken advantage of. Then seeing his opening, the dragon moved in. Using his sword in his right hand he pushed aside his opponent's weapon while launching his shoulder into the others shield forcing him back. The unexpected move surprised the bigger man setting him off balance. Taking advantage Dram brought his left sword up pinning his opponent's sword between his. With a quick twist of his wrists sent the bigger mans sword spinning out of his hand. Now Dram stood between his adversary and his weapon.

"Finally, I have won a match" Dram breathlessly shouted to the larger man in front of him.

Bowlsy only grinned as he spun low to the ground, using the centrifugal force, threw the shield at the dragon. The heavy flying disc hit Dram square in the chest nearly lifting him off the ground, making him take a step back while dropping his swords. Without hesitation Bowlsy quickly followed, grabbing the back of the shield flipped it upwards and smashed it into the dragon's face sending him to the ground. It was all Dram could do to keep it from getting squashed as he rolled out from under the weight of his opponent and his shield. Bowlsy tucked into a summersault grabbing the shield strap and yanked it off the dragon. Stunned Dram tried to reach for his swords only to find Bowlsy had recovered his and now held it over the dragon's head.

"You still have yet to win a match from me, little man, although that maneuver almost had me," Bowlsy said with an infectious laugh.

Dram laid back on the soft dirt as Bowlsy went on about the tactic. "Never try to take anything head-on in a battle. Avoid and if you can't, deflect. Your more experienced fighters will use distraction as I did with the shield while the real threat comes from a different direction."

Bowlsy extended his hand and helped Dram to his feet. "Don't be so hard on yourself my friend. Although we seem of the same age, I was trained in the art of warcraft from before I could walk. While other kids were out playing games, my father had me in the arena training for hours."

"Then why are you not out leading some army or another, that has got to be better pay and lodgings than this." Dram motioned to the other side of the road where the mercs had assembled for dinner.

Bowlsy slapped his new friend on the back and laughed pushing him towards the food. "Freedom and adventure my little friend, there is nothing like it for no amount of pay." Before Dram could even comment Bowlsy was off on another story. "There was this time off the coast of Spain. We were escorting a ship into the Mediterranean......"

Dram casually listened to the story as he studied the camp before him. These weren't just seasoned veterans, experienced from years of fighting. From the selecting back at the staging grounds, these were the best of what was available in times when there was a lot of mercs out of work. And now they were going to be taken somewhere and forged into a weapon against his own race.

"And so, with one hand I flung the pirate overboard to join his friends to swim back to whatever dung hole they crawled out of." Bowlsy's laugh was infectious as several of the mercs listening to the story joined in bringing the dragon out of his introspection.

"Come, let's get some food then, your story has given me quite the appetite." Dram said as he pushed his big friend in the direction of the cook wagon before he tried to start another story.

After getting their food they sat at one of the campfires with several other mercs. The dragon kept mostly to himself while eating his food, listening to the conversations surrounding him. Most of the talk was of home or of mutual acquaintances, but one conversation caught his attention though.

"We must be near our destination, it has been four days since we left," said a scruffy bearded man with an eastern accent.

"True," said another merc. "We must be headed to the northern territories."

A third man chimed in. "I grew up in these parts and the only thing ahead of us is an old burned down garrison. We must be taking the northern road to one of the other territories, there isn't anything around this area unless they built something new I don't know about. It has been a few years since I have been back."

Cold darkness started to creep into Dram as the merc mentioned the garrison, overriding his caution. "A burned-out garrison? Isn't that sort of rare?"

The local man's face lit up as he was eager to tell the story. "It was over twenty years ago, I was a boy of about ten. The area was pretty tame and there wasn't much need for protection except for some highway bandits and such. I was told the fort had a skeleton crew, just enough to keep the local troublemakers honest."

By this time several more mercs had gathered around the fire to hear the story of the local area. "So as the story goes there was a big to do a couple days before the fire. Troops were coming and going along the roads, but no one knew what they were up to or where they were going."

"Come on you really expect us to believe that?" chided one of the men near the campfire and was quickly hushed by his comrades. The local man looked around the group for more interruptions and then continued his story.

"The night of the fire, those that lived near the garrison said they could hear inhuman screams coming from the direction of the compound. Only one man was brave enough to go out into the night and check out what was going on."

The man paused to see how he was holding his audience. He had obviously told this story before and knew how to let the suspense build. Somehow the uncertainty of where they were all going helped catch the attention of the men.

"The next morning, several of the local villagers went out to investigate what went on. All they found left of the garrison was charred rubble. The fire was so hot that it even melted the stones of the central keep. Nothing was left, no bodies, no soldiers, nothing. The only thing that resembled what the garrison were parts of the outer wall, though I was told that was hard to identify as well." Again, the storyteller paused to let his audience digest the tale.

"Now my people are not superstitious nor are they fearful of anything but the most dangerous threats. That being said, after seeing what happened to the garrison the next morning, not one person went back. The next day soldiers from the neighboring territories showed up and sealed off the area. A week later and they left never to rebuild the fort."

Dram watched the people around the campfire listening to the story. He could tell that each person believed a different amount of the tale, then the narrator continued.

"I have seen some things in my time, as we all have in our profession. I never went and saw the ruins right after the fire happened, but I did a couple of years later. After two years there was still only black charred rock, nothing grew inside the walls. It was like it was cursed, after seeing that it's hard to be scared by much else."

Dram leaned closer to the local man. "You mentioned someone was brave enough to check out the fire that night, what happened of him?"

"I was pretty young at the time, but I remember my father talking about him with a bit of a laugh. I thought it a strange thing for such a disaster." The man paused as if he was trying to remember the events of his childhood. "The man wasn't all there to begin with, my father would say. That this was just the push he needed to really go crazy. I don't think what he said had any bearing but to confirm that the place was haunted. The man disappeared the next day, we were never sure if the soldiers took him or if he just wandered off."

Dram's was nearing his patience when he felt a tight hand clamping on his shoulder. Bowlsy could see his frustration and tried to intercept, why the dragon was not sure.

"Come on man what did the guy say he saw?" Bowlsy chimed in, also impatient with the story being drawn out.

"From what I am told, he said a great demon rose out of the inferno riding on golden flames and flew out into the night. I think that is why my father always chuckled when he mentioned the man. Nothing could have withstood the heat of that fire except something spawned from hell itself. He said if that was the case, it would be flying down not up. My father tended to have the worst jokes in the best of situations."

The men listening to the story erupted into a burst of laughter at the joke. The crowd started to disperse as it was getting to be time to turn in.

"Well, I have had about as much as I can eat." Bowlsy rose from his seat and started to head over to the wagon where they stored their gear.

"I'll head over in a minute, still trying to figure out how to beat you the next fight," said Dram with a sly grin.

"Well don't take all night." Said the big man. "We have a long way to go tomorrow and it's hard to sleep in those wagons."

Dram snorted disgust at Bowlsy's boasting as his friend walked off. Worst was that it was true.

Five days went fast as Bowlsy taught Dram different ways to fight while they traveled. The wagons weren't as cramped as when they first came to the staging ground allowing them some room to move around. At night, they practiced what they went over during the day on the trip. Dram always the good student picked it up fast, becoming almost a master at both shield and sword styles.

They were told tomorrow they would arrive at what would be their new home for the next several months. Dram would have to leave before that. He couldn't chance trying to escape from an encampment, especially one filled with dragon slayers.

Waiting until after midnight, Dram snuck out of the makeshift camp they had made for the night. Careful not to wake anyone, the mercs slept where ever was convenient. Most men bunked in or under the wagons while others kept near the fires, there was still an unexpected body sleeping in an unforeseen place. There were no guards on duty, since who would attack a group of over one hundred mercs.

Dram moved into the trees, making no sound. Every few seconds he would stop listening for anyone following. Thinking he had evaded any detection, he heard a voice.

"So, this is a little far out to be relieving yourself isn't it?" Spinning around Dram found Bowlsy not five feet behind him.

"Don't try to stop me. I don't want to hurt you."

With a chuckle, Bowlsy said, "I've seen you fight Nuis, don't think that will be a problem." Again, he had the same wide smile, drawing his dagger. Before Dram could draw his sword, he turned and threw the knife into the woods behind them. A short cry, then a figure fell forward out from behind the tree. It was one of the men at the table from the first meeting. Bowlsy retrieved his knife after making sure he was dead.

"Thanks, I didn't know he was there."

"Seems we need to work on your wood skills next we meet, dragon."

Dram's sword was out and touching Bowlsy's throat, but he didn't flinch at all. "Ya, I know what you are. I knew the moment I walked into that tavern. Don't worry though for I am probably the only one in these parts that could recognize a dragon in human form."

"My people are the Skald and friends to your kind far to the north across the sea. We heard about a great battle between dragons and men a few years ago. In fact, that battle happened in the place these mercs seem to be heading."

Dram only nodded, he also knew where they were headed. Greytock, they were making a beeline right for it. He pondered to himself if this nightmare would never end.

Bowlsy cut in on Dram's thoughts "Look, no one hires mercs in the onset of winter unless they have one thing in mind. They are going to train those guys till spring, then unleash their plan. For years, I have been trying to infiltrate their organization, but I have to get back and report what I have learned. I imagine you do also."

"First I have to check on a friend, if the mercs are heading to Greytock, then more people are involved than I first thought."

"Then take care, my friend, remember you have allies to the north, both your kin and mine."

By the time, Dram resheathed his sword Bowlsy had disappeared. What friends we make in this world he pondered. Finding a clearing big enough, Dram released his magic, once again taking dragon form. Launching up into the night, he headed for Greytock.

Garath and Danielle galloped down the dusty road leading to the northwest. The leaves had changed color weeks ago and were now falling, covering the road. Six guards followed them, ones personally checked for loyalty by the bench in the garden including Captain Norjor.

Holding up her hand to stop, the small group reigned in their mounts. "The horses need to rest, let's stop for breakfast." The guards dismounted walking the animals over to a small stream that followed the road. They had been riding hard for four hours now since they had left the capital at dawn. It would take three days at this pace to reach the northern territories where Danielle thought her brother might be.

Danielle had made it clear to her guards that Garath was a special friend of hers and that they were to be left alone whenever possible. It wasn't uncommon for a noble lady to take a courtier, whether proper or not, no one would mention a word. Nobles were for nobles to deal with and the guards would do their duty to protect their princess.

"How does it feel to be back outside? I know this isn't what you are used to but must be some comfort not to be so confined."

Garath had to think about his answer, although not the majestic peaks he was used to, the dragon found the situation he as in very compelling. "Besides everything that has been going on, I am really enjoying it. The only thing is all the talking, a person can barely think."

"I can have you sit with the guards if that's better for you."

"Oh, I think I am pretty good right where I am, I am supposed to be protecting you." Garath's sense of humor always present, they continued their discussion through the meal. When finished she signaled for the guards to get ready. One guard brought their horses over, mounting up they were again galloping down the road heading to the north.

The small group stopped at a clearing next to the road. Dismounting they unpacked the supplies and started to prepare for lunch. While Danielle and Garath started to eat the six guards started into practice exercises.

Garath turned to Danielle confused. "Wow, those guys have some stamina, riding for half the day and still taking time for sword practice?"

Danielle laughed at the dragon's remark knowing that he would easily be able to take on any of her guards. Overhearing their conversation, Norjor stopped his practice and walked over to the young couple. "You should join us Garath, the exercise loosens up the muscles and makes riding easier. Otherwise, at the end of the day, you could be so sore that you won't even sleep. Not to mention we might need your sword in case we get into some trouble." The last he said with a bit of sarcasm not lost on the dragon.

Garath tried to turn down the invitation but Danielle was having too much fun with the situation.

"Go on Garath, I'm sure you can learn a thing or two. Just in case we get into some trouble." Danielle said as she pushed the dragon towards where the guards were training. Norjor nodded to one of his men to give Garath his practice sword.

"These are blunted so the only real danger is a bruise, just keep them away from the face. We are not trying to kill each other but an unlucky shot can happen." Norjor's tone was almost condescending but still friendly enough. Garath understood that being seen as with the princess put him in a position that wasn't a threat but worse, a fluff.

"I'm sure you know how to use a sword Garath, but have you had any formal training?" Now the tone was sincere. Garath had a sense he could be honest with the captain.

"Nothing formal, just some tips here and there from friends who have been in the military."

The two men squared off in the center of the makeshift ring that the guards had set up. "Here is your first tip, unless you have a shield, never stand with your full front to your opponent." Without warning, Norjor struck at Garath at his unprotected side. At the last second, the captain turned his blade hitting the dragon with the flat on his still injured left arm. The blow wasn't hard, but the pain clearly flashed across his face.

"Come on Garath, that wasn't that hard." The dragon immediately stood to position and steadied his sword. With a smile, he replied to the captain, "Let's do this again."

The fight only lasted a few seconds with Norjor clearly being a far better swordsman. Garath not wanting to give himself away couldn't use his dragon strength or speed. Soon the dragon was disarmed and staring down the point of the captain's sword. Moving swiftly, he slid in and to his left, using his right forearm to push away Norjor's sword. From the blade, he moved his arm across the captain's chest as his momentum brought him to the side of his opponent. Surprised, Norjor tried to turn to face the dragon but the move was keeping him looking away. Placing his right foot behind the captain's legs Garath pushed backwards with his right hand sending the captain flying across his right leg. The force sent the captain flying back onto the ground knocking the wind out of him.

The other guards moved forward as Norjor held up his hand catching his breath and letting out a gasping laugh. "Guess I deserved that, nice move Garath."

The dragon extended his hand to the experienced officer. "Sorry, it was the only thing I could think of after you disarmed me."

"After you almost dropped your sword from the first hit, I was surprised you came back so strong."

At the last comment, Danielle had to put in a word. "You know captain, Garath has a nasty gash through his left arm. One he got from rescuing me."

"No, I didn't, sorry Garath. You have a lot of natural ability. If you want I can help you out with some of your swordsmanship."

Garath nodded in agreement at the proposal and they all moved back to where the food had been prepared. This time Danielle and Garath ate with the rest of the guards. Once finished they left with a new comradery to the group.

The sun was just starting to set over the mountains when they decided to stop for the night. Although it wasn't raining they went ahead and pitched tents and started a fire to cook their dinner. Trail rations where all they had but two of the guards took off to the woods to see if any game was about. Just before dark, they came back with a brace of pheasants and a small pig. The game wasn't big this close to the capital. Mostly hunted out but there was plenty of smaller animals that most didn't bother with.

Once again, Danielle and Garath sat removed from the guards as they ate their meal. Talks of wonders in both worlds were exchanged, although if overheard would sound like two different countries, not two races. The night waned as they decided to head to bed, the guards all asleep, but for the one keeping watch. There shouldn't be any danger this close to the capital, but with recent events, it would pay to be careful.

A scream woke Garath in the middle of the night. Crawling out of his tent he could hear crying coming from inside of Danielle's. Panicked he rushed over and threw open the flap as he shouted her name. Using his inner sight, he could tell she was the only one in the tent. Hearing Garath's voice, she crawled to him and flung her arms around his neck, hugging him tightly. Tears and sobbing burst from her as they realized it was a nightmare and no real threat. Garath waved the guards back, assuring them she was ok with his gesture. Gently he stroked the back of her head assuring her that everything was all right.

The sobbing ceased, then so did the tears, as she once again looked up into Garath's eyes. So close to her, she could make them out with the glow of the harvest moon.

"I'm sorry, I am such a wreck. This is all so overwhelming."

"Shhh, you have been through more in the last week than most have been through in a lifetime. You deserve to be a lunatic." Danielle playfully hit Garath in the chest with the last comment.

"I said wreck not a lunatic!" she laughed as she again curled up into Garath's embrace. For the first time in weeks, she felt safe, buried in his arms. The guards moved back to their tents to try to get some rest. It was going to be another long day of riding tomorrow.

Garath tried to let Danielle lay back down but she clung to him tighter "Don't go, I don't want to be alone, please." Her plea sent a strange pain though Garath, almost an ache. He didn't understand it, but at that moment he would do anything for this woman. Gently they both lay down inside the small tent, barely enough room for either of them. Still curled in his arms she fell fast asleep while Garath pondered this new feeling he had. He was still awake when the predawn came and the guards started getting the camp ready to leave. Not wanting to wake her yet he slipped out of the tent to help prepare for the day.

Two more days passed as they traveled. Each night Garath stayed with Danielle, while the guards said nothing. The gold dragon still pondered the strange new feelings he had but enjoyed their time together even more. Something about holding her soft body against his all night aroused more than just excitement in him. Although impossible to act on, it still felt good to have her heart beating next to his, her warm breath on his neck.

Three vassals ran the northern territories, spread from the northeast to the northwest. Danielle had been in the northeast province when she was attacked. That was from where her brother had left for the other vassal estates. He would be in either the northwest or north. They were headed for the northwest area first. This was the most likely area that they would find him. If not there, they would start for the north keep, along the most likely route that her brother would travel from.

Still half a day out from the northwest keep, they came to a crossroads with a small guard shack. The new road ran between the northern provinces connecting the keeps. Three guards stood duty at the post as the party rode up. Seeing the royal crest on group's uniforms, they quickly asked to be of help. After a brief conversation, they were told that her brother's caravan had not been by but that they were expecting it. They rested the mounts while getting some fresh supplies, being caught up on local events. Soon they were on the road again heading to the northern keep, another full day ride.

Still a half a day's ride from the northern keep, they reigned into camp for the night. Danielle and Garath walked together holding hands into the woods. Leaves covered the ground, as the only trees still holding any colors were the pine and firs, which stayed green all year round.

"I must transform soon, I can't show up in human form to talk to your brother."

"I have been thinking about this too, although I haven't wanted you to go yet." Since the nightmare, the two of them had been inseparable, growing closer. Each night they spent together, held in Garath's arms was the only sleep she got. "In the morning I will send you on an errand back to the northwest keep. The guards will think I am either tired of you or sending you away under a pretext, that I am trying to save your hide from my brother. Either way, you should be able to follow us. I will try to set up a meeting with my brother and when ready you two can meet. This is the only way I can think of to even work out some form a truce between our two peoples."

"If that's the case, how about giving me your worst mount in the morning." Puzzled by the remark, Danielle could only guess at what he had in mind.

The conversation turned to less important events as they continued their walk back to the camp. The guards had three large rabbits cooking over the fire, the game was far more plentiful up here in the north. After dinner, they all turned in with Garath again joining Danielle in her tent.

Holding her in his arms, Garath thought she would again fall asleep. However, tonight was different. Caressing his cheek, she slid up so that their faces were close together. Softly she pressed her lips to his, pursed and firm. Garath had never kissed in any form before. Dragons don't have the same show of affection as humans do. In fact, in only special circumstances, do they even show any affection. Mating was one thing, but this was something entirely different, something memorable.

Sensing Garath's hesitation, she stopped, but he continued pulling her closer in his arms. His kisses were returned as they caressed each other in turn. Finally nuzzling her face into Garath's neck, she quickly fell asleep, soon after he slept also dreaming of this new connection with Danielle.

The next morning Danielle announced that Garath would be heading back to the northwest keep with a message. If the guards didn't believe her, they showed none of it. Garath pulled Norjor aside, the captain of the guard. "Take care of her, there are things going on that neither of us knows fully about."

"Take care of yourself Garath, it's been good traveling with you." Motioning for a guard to bring his horse, Garath mounted up. Checking his supplies, he took one last look at Danielle and spurred his horse into a gallop, heading back the way they had come. The rest of the party saddled up and started down the road to the northern keep.

An hour later, Garath decided he was far enough away from the party. Turning off the road Garath looked for a rocky place where he could change and eat without leaving tracks. Around midday, he came across the stream he had noticed before. Nearly a wingspan across it was almost a small river. Dry bedrock bordered it on both sides providing ample room to eat. Removing the tack and saddle from the horse, he hid them in the bushes. He knew the horse might run when he transformed so he tied him to a tree overhanging a shallow part of the stream. He didn't want to use the horse for a meal, but he needed to move fast. Although a dragon can fly much faster than a horse can run, it was not so fast that he could waste any more time before he tried to catch up to the party. There being only one road to the north keep made it easier but still, he could not delay.

Garath released his magic in the middle of the stream. A slight sound of rushing air, as where once a man stood was now a golden dragon, twenty feet high. The horse barely screamed as Garath quickly broke its neck. The meal was stringy but filling. Feeling his strength return he made sure all the remains and blood washed down the stream. The fish and other creatures in the water would make short work of what was left of his meal, leaving very little for anyone to even recognize what kind of animal it was.

It was well past midday; Garath took a long cool drink of water from the stream. The trees hid him for now but not when he took off. He would have to fly low over the forest hoping they would hide his flight as he tried to follow the road back to Danielle and her group. Launching out of the water he brought his wings down hard to capture the wind and lift his massive body. Cresting the trees, he headed to the east, paralleling the road that he hoped would lead him to the end of his mission.

Back down the road to the west, a single figure on horseback watched the forest ahead from a rise in the path. A newly healed scar ran down his left cheek from below his eye to his shoulder. He watches as a golden dragon flew up out of the woods and headed to the east. "What are you up to dragon and where is your friend?" he asked himself. Looking down at the tracks he had been following for several days, he pushed his horse into a gallop.

CHAPTER 9

Danielle's party reached the gates of the keep around sundown. Strangely quiet was the activity in the surrounding area. The soldiers at the outlying guard shacks were of little information except that indeed her brother was still at the fort.

"I am here to see my brother Lord Lombard," she told the guards at the gate. The six soldiers with her and the family crest got instant attention.

"Please come on through, I will have a message sent to him immediately."

Danielle's party rode under the gate and into the first bailey just as her brother came running out of the main doors to the keep. "Danielle, what are you doing here?"

"Jerome, we need to talk, quietly." Dismounting she gave the reigns to Norjor as her brother led her inside. They went through several hallways until he opened a door to what could only be called an office. As they entered, she noticed several chairs surrounding a table in the middle with maps and papers scattered all about it.

"This is about as quiet as we can get, so what has you here, with very little escort and actually riding a horse?"

"There is no easy way to say this. Father is gone. He survived the journey back but passed away suddenly. I think you are in danger also." Danielle could not impress enough on him how much danger they were in. He just smiled and put his hands on her shoulders, as if he was talking to a little girl with big delusions.

"Come on sis, I am sorry our father is gone, but I was there when he was injured. It was an accident; there is no danger in that except that our prey got a lucky shot in. I am surprised he made it back home with how deep that wound was. That's why we sent him there in the first place, our surgeon didn't have the skill to properly heal him, and not sure any did."

Danielle was getting annoyed at being dismissed so easily. "Listen to me! my convoy was attacked, our uncle is dead, I barely escaped to make it back home." Danielle told him the story of how she made it back to the capital with the help of two strangers, leaving out the part about them being dragons. He listened intently, not interrupting until she was finished.

"Where are these two saviors? I would like to reward them. It must have been a hard journey to make it back to the capital." His voice held a genuine concern, for no matter how dramatic he thought his sister might be, there was a lot to her story. If even part of it was true, it was completely amazing.

"One stayed in the capital on business, the other I sent to the northwest province on a pretend errand." Danielle seemed to dismiss them as mere servants.

"Oh? Tired of him already, were you?" Jerome teased, causing Danielle's annoyance to increase.

"Kind of. It was one thing to have to get rescued by a stranger, but another for him to volunteer to accompany us up here. He was like a lap dog trying to cater to my every whim. I figured you wouldn't care if I had a little distraction, father might have, but I'm a big girl now." She said as she tried to play off the brief affair as one of just amusement.

"Well seems you have grown up, and no I wouldn't ever dream of getting in the way of your fun." The last was said with a certain irony. "I always felt sorry for all the nursemaids and guards that father appointed to keep you reigned in. It never seemed to work, you always found a way to get out and get into trouble. Of course, this is the first time a man has been involved." Danielle blushed as her brother teased her. Only family can make remarks that hit home like that.

146

Seeing his sister's discomfort, he said, "Come with me I have something to show you, it won't bring back father but may console you some."

Jerome led Danielle out of the office and to the back of the keep. The castle was not large by any means, more of a fortress built to house soldiers and a base of operations. Jerome opened a door that passed through to the rear courtyard. Torches lit the area revealing large wooden walls lining the stone floor. Each wood panel was engraved with the same strange symbols that were on the bench in the garden at home. Peering into the darkness she could make out a large shape huddled in the corner. It moved as they walked out on the stone balcony that overlooked the area. Danielle gasped as she finally realized what it was. Lying on the rocky ground of the courtyard was a dragon.

Garath caught up to the group right before sunset. The forest was thick north of the road for a half mile until a large rock face jetted upwards several hundred feet. On top of this ridge, Garath watched the group work their way around the mountain along the road and into a small valley. The path ended into a large fortress at the other end. Garath's heart jumped into his throat as he realized where he was. He had been flying low all this time and really didn't watch the landmarks, trying to catch Danielle's group before dusk. Now he stared at the rebuilt fortress known to the dragons as Greytock.

"Don't be afraid, we are perfectly safe. The wards set around the courtyard keep the dragon contained. Some even keep it from using its magic if I want." Jerome said

147

proudly as if he lit more torches to push away the darkness.

"This is the creature that killed our father, and I can give you the revenge you so rightly deserve." Still in shock, as she was still trying to contemplate the scene in front of her, Jerome handed her a crossbow. Not knowing why, she grabbed it, feeling its smooth hardwood stock, although big for her hands. Anger flared at what this beast had done to her father; slowly she raised the weapon to point at the captured dragon cowardly crouching in the corner.

"We tracked this one to a high ledge after killing one of our livestock. It ran, we had to surround it in the valley below. It then tried to escape and that's when our father was attacked. We were able to capture it instead and brought it here."

"So, it was just trying to defend itself, after you hunted it down for killing what, a cow, some pig?" Lowering the crossbow, Danielle's anger turned to sorrow for the poor beast. "It was just hungry, that's all." She let the crossbow drop from her hands, as she now understood some of the plight Garath's people were going through.

Jerome slowly picked up the crossbow from the stone slab as Danielle moved closer to the edge of the high balcony. The dragon didn't move from the corner on the far side of the yard, afraid of something. The torches were not bright enough to see the dragon clearly, but she knew that it had been here for a while. Enough to break its spirit like a cowering dog.

"I knew you were a bleeding heart like father, why didn't you just die like you were supposed to?" Danielle whipped around at her brother's remark, too stunned to speak. Jerome held the crossbow pointed at her chest.

148

"Do you know how much trouble it was to have my men open up a path just right that the dragon would have no choice but to attack our father, then to coordinate it with your death? I spent years planning this. Just to get father to go hunting with me I had to make promises for the future that I never planned on keeping."

"But why? You were already taking over, you were soon to be Duke!" Danielle screamed at her brother as anger again filled her at the betrayal of her family.

"Why do you think, you were too young to remember but you still sided with father on all subjects. I was there when the dragons attacked this keep, in his wisdom grandfather knew they were coming. He hid me up the mountain and told me no matter what happened to hide until he came to get me. I watched as the keep burned, no one survived, not even our grandfather. For two days, I waited until reinforcements arrived, I was only ten years old, but I remember everything. They took me back to the capital where I told father what had happened. All he said was that grandfather brought it on himself. Can you believe that, his own father?" The anger was filling Jerome to the point of shaking, but he calmed himself and continued in a cool voice.

"Grandfather was genius at hunting dragons. He even developed a poison for them called dragon's bane. The first time it was tested was at that battle, but even that didn't help much. Now my friends and I have perfected it to where it should kill a dragon with one shot. This crossbow has that poison on it, and this is the test we have been waiting for."

"Wait, I have been talking to the dragons. They want peace, to stop the killing. You can't do this, it will stop any agreements we can come together on." Danielle over the initial shock was determined to try to salvage something from this.

"Then you are a sympathizer, I knew you would be on their side just like father!" Again, the anger filled Jerome, nothing would stop him from avenging his grandfather.

"No, listen to me. We can stop all the killing on both sides. We can leave each other in peace." Danielle's pleas fell on deaf ears, as Jerome's anger consumed him.

"I knew you were too weak to help me in this. Even as Duke, you and father would have tried to stop me, like you are trying to do now. There is no compromise with this evil, so they must be exterminated. Like this!"

With his last statement, Jerome aimed the crossbow at the dragon in the courtyard. Squeezing the trigger, he let the bolt loose, time seemed to stand still as all his plans were finally coming together. He was going to avenge his grandfather. He was going to destroy all the dragons. Too focused on his prey, Jerome didn't notice as Danielle jumped in front of the crossbow until it was too late. The bolt hit her in the shoulder, knocking her off into the courtyard below. The hard ground slammed the air out of her lungs along with the piercing pain of the crossbow bolt.

Jerome just looked down at her shaking his head. "I have more of those you know, that was just foolish."

Catching her breath, she could only think of one thing. Inhaling deeply, she screamed "Garath!"

Once the party had headed inside, Garath headed around to the back of the fortress. The cover of night helped conceal his golden skin. He could see a lot of torches lit, but little activity in the keep as a whole. Something was strange though. Using his senses, he could make out the

150

people of the keep, except for the area in the back. It was as if something was blocking his magic, or something was blocking all magic. He could only be ready if Danielle called, to talk truce he hoped, but something told him he was here to fight.

"Garath!" screamed in his mind. It was Danielle, more in his head than hearing her. No dragon had ever mind spoke to a human before, not that he had ever heard. He didn't have time to contemplate it, as he knew she needed him.

The wall to the back of the keep was only a few wingspans away, with his senses he couldn't detect her in any other part of the fortress, so this must be where she was. With a few quick pounces, he was up and gliding over the low keep walls. Folding his wings, he landed hard on the stone floor of the back courtyard. He could see Danielle lying on the ground before him but there was a presence, another dragon. Turning behind him, he saw the crouching form of Lo'Lith. Shock filled his mind, he could only stand there and look between his kin and Danielle. Reflexes took over as he turned to face the man standing on the stone balcony ten feet above the courtyard.

"Blacroaker, we have company!" Jerome shouted while reloading his crossbow. Seconds later a man in a blue robe came out of a door on the other side of the balcony. Runes filled his clothes along with something in his hand. Garath couldn't make it out but he could see the pulsing glow of power it held.

Garath roared a challenge at the two men but they both laughed. "I don't think so dragon, you are in our trap." Then the Magi pointed the device in his hands at the dragon and lightning shot out of it striking him in the left shoulder. Pain nearly crippled him as his skin blistered from the impact. In reflex, he inhaled and breathed his fire at the two men on the stone. An invisible wall stopped his flame and shot it in all directions. Stopping immediately for fear of hitting Danielle he ran over to grab her body and move it to safety. Again, the wizard shot lightning, this time hitting Garath in the back nearly paralyzing him. Limping back to Lo'Lith, he gently dropped her body at the dragon's feet. *"Protect her,"* he said in mind speak. Turning his attention back to the two men, he decided if his flame didn't work then maybe his body would.

Charging the balcony, Garath launched his weight into the wall under the two men shoulder first. They may block his magic, but they couldn't block the full weight of a dragon. The wall shook but Garath bounced off the shield like a stone cliff. He couldn't take another hit like that, his shoulder nearly dislocated on that attempt and nothing happened.

Jerome has loaded the crossbow again with another bolt. A smile on the face of the wizard infuriated Garath. This man was having fun. Focusing his power, he launched an all-out attack on the shield with his fire, willing it to burn hotter than he ever had before. The wizard just stood and laughed.

"You will need more than that dragon to best my defenses. Now I am done playing with you. Let's test this my lord." Jerome's only agreement was firing the crossbow at Garath. He wasn't afraid of a little arrow but something in his mind made him duck as the bold flew overhead, embedding into the wooden siding on the wall.

"Dammit, was trying for a head shot. Give me another arrow." Blacroaker handed Jerome another bolt as he tried to reset the crossbow. Not waiting for his lord, the magi unleashed another lightning strike into Garath, this time hitting his left flank. Garath roared as he collapsed, his back leg too numb, making him unable to stand. The two men up on the balcony were unharmed. Rage filled him as he tried to protect both Danielle and Lo'Lith.

Jerome turned to Blacroaker "It's jammed, it won't hold the bowstring. I can't restring it." Unable to reload the crossbow he turned to his mage. "Finish the new one; we still need to test the dragonsbane. And finish my sister while you are at it." A nod from the wizard was all it took as he turned to the dragons. "Feel my power beast, or at least the power I have channeled from one of your own." The item that the magi held in his hand resembled a dragon's talon. However, the dragon's graveyard kept any dragon body parts from being used in such a way. It was impossible that this wizard was able to get what he had in his hands. Then the dread hit him, turning he looked at Lo'Lith, her third talon was missing from her right claw. The humans had found a way to use dragon power by not killing the dragon itself. Renewed rage forced him to try again to kill the duo, but another lightning strike dropped him to the ground.

"Come on dragon, you really think you can best a magus? In my own home?" The words cut like a blade into Garath's soul. Nothing he did could even make an impact. What else could he do? Again, the lightning struck, this time in the chest numbing most of his body.

Dram was almost to Greytock, the flight was longer than he first would have thought. Not used to this part of the country it took him a while to get his bearings. Now he was flying high above what the humans called the north

153

road that led to the fortress itself. The sun had set almost an hour ago but there was still the faint light coming from the horizon.

Clearing the last ridge, Dram could now view Greytock. Even in the dark, he could see the fortress, rebuilt from the last time he was here. Something flashed in the back courtyard drawing his attention. The main part of the keep still blocked his view so he circled around for a better look.

Astonishment struck him as the main body of the fortress cleared and he could see fully into the back courtyard. Garath was standing in the middle of the yard between another dragon and a blue-robed magus. Garath lashed out with his fire but it only bounced off an invisible wall, while the wizard returned fire with lightning bolts out of an item in his hand. His friend was taking the worst of the battle.

Dram couldn't rush in. Two dragons already were under this magi's control. Looking over the courtyard, he noticed the wooden panels lining the walls. With his inner site, he could see the power they held, or more accurately, the power they could contain between them. Someone had channeled the life force in the wood itself, no wonder the mage was winning this battle. A plan started forming in his mind as he dropped low barely skimming the ground as he flew down the mountain slope behind the fortress.

Reaching the wall, he pulled up, clearing the twenty-foot high walls and hovered over the magi himself. Dram released a deafening roar to get the magi's attention. Both humans jumped at the site of another dragon, but quickly composed themselves. "Blacroaker, handle these, I am going to get more men." Jerome turned and headed in the door behind the balcony.

The wizard turned to Dram smiling. "Come on dragon, I have plenty for all of you!" Delighting in his own power, he aimed the weapon in his hand at Dram. Not hesitating, he unleashed his own breath weapon. Green acid blasted from his mouth bouncing off the invisible shield, dripping down to the rock below. The wizard just laughed at Dram's foolish attempt.

"You can't harm me you fool. We have been ready for you for a long time." Raising the weapon in his hand again, he shot a bolt of lightning hitting Dram in the shoulder. Pain exploded through his eyes, but he kept focus on the shield around the magi. More acid shot out of Dram's mouth, completely covering the magical shield. Too late the wizard realized what the dragon was doing. The acid had dripped down the shield and started burning the rock beneath. The wizard now completely surrounded by a pool of the deadly liquid began flowing under the magical barrier.

Screams filled the night as the acid crept closer to the magi, starting to burn his robe. The pool now completely engulfed the balcony leaving nowhere for the man to run. Again, he screamed as the acid burned his feet and the rock itself. Dram kept more acid coming until there were no more sounds from the human magi.

Garath was just getting to his feet. Still wounded the magical energy was finally wearing off. Dram turned still hovering in the air, took careful aim, as he burned the runic inscribed wood panels on the far side of the courtyard from his friends. Without all the panels in place, the containment magic lost its effect.

Arrows hit Dram, penetrating his hard armor. The guards from the front of the keep were now within bow range. "Garath we must go, I will get Danielle."

"No! I will get her." Garath moved to pick up Danielle in his massive front arms. He ignored the pain that still shot through his body. Holding tight to her frail body, he launched over the back of the keep wall into flight.

For the first time, Dram recognized Lo'Lith, still cowering in the corner of the courtyard. "Move Now!" Dram blasted more acid in the direction of the incoming guards. They were still too far out of range, but it slowed them down some.

Lo'Lith still hadn't moved from the corner. Dram could not understand why she did not go, and then he understood. The panels he destroyed did more than just contain magic it also was a cage.

"Lo'Lith, the walls are gone. Please get out of here." Dram pleaded, he would not leave her behind. More arrows hit him as he waited for the other dragon to take off. Finally, she leaped over the wall as if testing if it were true. Once outside she leaped again into flight heading after Garath.

Small points of pain reminded Dram of the guards still coming at him. These arrows should not be penetrating his armor, but somehow, they were cutting through him as if he wore none at all. More of an annoyance really, if they did hit a sensitive part it could be bad. Firing one more jet of acid he turned and leaped into flight following his friends.

Garath was having trouble, he was badly wounded and trying to hold Danielle was getting difficult.

"Let me help, you are too wounded to fly both of you." Garath could not argue as Dram flew in under his friend

with his back directly below Danielle. Garath slowly dropped her onto the broad black shoulders, her unconscious body lying limp between the massive wings. A soft orange glow surrounded her as Dram used his magic to keep her warm.

"Come on we have to go to the Council, they need to know what is going on." A slight glow covered each of the dragons as they augmented their speed with magic. Time was of the essence as they headed for home.

"Come in Shurlok, glad you finally made it," said Jerome as the man with a scar running down his left cheek walked into his office.

"I hear you had some interesting guests recently, in fact, ones I have been tracking since the attack on your sister. If it hadn't been for this medallion I might not be here today. I wasn't planning on their intervention or I would have brought more enchantments." Shurlok fingered a leather necklace inscribed with runes that hid him from dragon magic.

Shurlok went over the past couple of weeks with Jerome. His fight with the golden dragon, the dragons changing to human form and the help his sister was giving them.

"Let's keep this to ourselves; the last thing we want is to have everyone suspected of being dragons. We can use the new dragonsbane to test our people. It won't hurt humans, so we can start mixing it in with the men's food. Any dragon spy will become immediately sick. Come I need to show you something."

Jerome led Shurlok out the front of the keep to the main courtyard. Wagons filled with men were just coming through the gate. "Over one hundred battle tested mercenaries, I need you to train them, train them to kill dragons."

"When did all this happen? I was only gone for three weeks."

"Sorry my friend, but there were plans in the works that I could not reveal to even my closest lieutenants until I took control of the country. Now that I have the rulership, we can move forward with nothing in our way." As Jerome talked, the last of the convoy entered the courtyard, they watched as the mercs stepped down from the wagons and gathered before the new Duke.

"Men, I am Duke Lombard. I have brought you all here for one mission. You are not soldiers any more but weapons. Ones that will be forged and sharpened with skills you never dreamed existed with one purpose. To not only kill dragons but to wipe them off the face of our world."

Mutters of awe and disbelief flowed through the crowd. They had heard this story before, but not from someone so high up. Having the ruler of the country confirm it gave it a completely new scope.

"This is your commander Shurlok, he answers only to me and I answer to no one. Once you are done with your training you will be the most skilled fighting force ever assembled. After our mission is done, you can take those skills and become the highest paid mercenaries in the country or if you prove yourselves worthy, you can join me as one of the knights of the Conclave.

"They are all yours, my friend, do what you do best." Shurlok only nodded as he started barking orders to the men on where to billet. The last pieces of his plan were falling into place.

"Sir, may I have a word with you?" Jerome turned to find Norjor standing at attention behind him. Nodding to the soldier, he continued.

"I want to help sir. Those beasts took lady Lombard, I want to see them dead. It was my duty to protect her!" Norjor nearly stumbled over the words then shouted as he tried to get them out.

Inwardly Jerome smiled; this was too good to be true. It had not occurred to him to use his sister's disappearance as motivation for his people.

"Granted, but I need you to take your men back to the capital and tell them what happened here. I will be along in a couple of weeks. When I am back, you can return here to train with the other recruits. You should not miss much as the first couple weeks of training will be what you already know as a soldier. Norjor nodded at the comment, turning he went to round up his men to return to the capital.

Jerome's inner smile turned to an outward grin. Twenty years he planned for this moment, now it was finally a reality. Come spring the dragons would be obliterated. Turning, he walked back into his office. There was still much to coordinate in the Conclave, he would have to have a new wizard transferred here to replace Blacroaker, in fact, he would have all the magi sent here to help with the training. They would also build the weapons and armor for his new army, ones magically enhanced specifically to fight dragons.

CHAPTER 10

The sun was just starting to break to the east as the three dragons neared the home of the Council, a large volcano still warm from activity. The peak of the mountain had collapsed leaving a large crater at the top almost two miles wide. A small forest covered one side of the depression while a rocky lake took up the other. Steam could be seen coming out of several smaller pools near the edge of the crater. The water ran from the smaller pools into the big lake then out into the forest below. Sheer cliffs lined the small valley on all sides making it near impossible to climb out. The steep slope of the mountain itself would keep any from climbing up to the ridgeline.

Dram landed near the opening to several caves a short distance from the small pools. Lightly touching down, he did his best not to damage his precious cargo. Garath and Lo'Lith were not so gentle, tired from their ordeal the night before and the long flight. Once regaining his balance, the golden dragon reached up and removed the small human from Dram's back.

"What is the meaning of this Dram? Humans are forbidden here." A silver dragon was standing at the mouth of a large cave. Age showed in his eyes and body, his horns and claws dulled by countless years.

"My apologies Speaker, we didn't have time to ask permission. She is badly injured and unconscious. She has no idea how we got here, there is a crossbow bolt in her shoulder."

"Then let me help." The old dragon, clearly displeased, waved his claw in front of the group. A green light formed a pallet of energy floating a few feet above the ground. Garath tried to lay Danielle on the hovering bed but soon as her blood came in contact with the green energy it dissolved leaving her limp form once again in his arms.

"Strange, something is disrupting my magic. Careful Garath, here try this." The elder dragon used his magic to raise a stone slab from the rocky ground. Again, the golden dragon tried to lay his friend on the makeshift bed, this time she stayed on it but Garath hovered over her just in case.

Lo'Lith came up to the unconscious women, sniffing at the arrow in her shoulder. "It's the poison on the arrow, the same that they used on me but stronger somehow. If it wasn't for her I would have that arrow in me, she jumped in the way to save me."

"Then we will do all in our power to help her." The silver dragon used his magic to raise the rock slab and moved it into the large cave. The dragons followed as they wound down several tunnels to a large room filled with tables of books and instruments. With a whisper from the elder dragon, lights sprang up along each wall, not a flame but something almost as bright as the sun.

Bringing the stone slab down to rest on the floor the old dragon started to examine the wound, careful not to touch any of the blood. "The arrow didn't go all the way through her shoulder which is unfortunate. It looks blocked by the bone, which can cause some problems. Dram can you take human form, I am going to need you for this."

Dram nodded as he started the transformation, seconds later the black dressed human form stood before the other dragons. "I want you to barely touch the arrow, wash your hand off in this if there are any ill effects." Magically a pale of water drifted over from one of the tables in the room coming to sit next to the rock slab. Hesitantly Dram moved over next to Danielle's still form. The bolt wasn't very big, only eighteen inches in length, far shorter than the arrows used by most of the soldiers. Slowly he pinched the arrow between his thumb and forefinger. Fire shot through his hand reflexively pulling it back, he jammed it into the bucket of water. The pain lessened but the burning still continued until he wiped his hands on the dirt floor trying to rub the poison off.

"It's worse than I thought, my apologies Dram, but it had to be tested." The silver dragon shook his head in confusion as he tried to contemplate what lied before him. "The poison, for lack of a better word is acidic to our magic. The water should have easily washed it off your hand but its concentration even with a mere touch is insurmountable. My guess is, if this arrow would have hit Lo'Lith, she would have been dead in seconds. Being that this young woman is still alive leads me to believe a reaction happens between the poison and our body chemistry. I will study it more later, let's get this thing out of her. I won't be able to use magic because of the poison, but I know a few tricks. Grab these please." Two items floated up off one of one of the tables and floated over to Dram. He had seen human blacksmiths use them when forging metal. One was a poker for stirring the coals the other tongs to grab hot metal out of the forge for hammering.

"Garath I need you to heat up the tip of that metal rod so that it glows red. When Dram pulls the arrow out with the tongs, I need you to push the hot end into the wound. No don't be shocked, the heat will instantly dry the blood sealing the wound, keeping her from getting weaker." The golden dragon nodded he understood although he didn't like the idea.

Dram handed the poker to Garath who grasped it in his claw. "Ready?" Garath focused his fire breath at the end of the poker trying to heat it up without melting it. His skin could resist the heat of his own flame but not the heated metal. "Let's hurry this is getting hot on the handle."

Quickly Dram moved over Danielle with the tongs ready to grasp the arrow. Taking hold of the projectile, he clamped the tongs together pinching it in between. Deftly he ripped the arrow out of her shoulder. "Now!" Garath moved in and touched the poker to the wound now oozing blood.

"Harder, you have to get it inside the wound or it can leave blood pooling under the skin." Garath cringed at the comment from the old dragon but did as he said. A quick scream escaped from Danielle from the pain, then she was once again unconscious.

"Dram, can you bring that arrow over here to the table and set it on this plate." The silver dragon pointed at a gold serving plate sitting on one of the tables. "The metal in the plate will not contaminate the poison. Hopefully her blood didn't change the chemistry either, so I can study it more."

"There is nothing more any of you can do now. I suggest you get some food and rest. The forest has plenty of game so feel free to help yourself. I will call a meeting of the Council tomorrow, let's hope that our new friend here is able to tell us something." Dram and Lo'Lith headed out of the room at the Speaker's suggestion while Garath stayed behind.

At a look from the silver dragon, Garath shook his head "I'm not hungry, I will stay with Danielle." Bowing his head in understanding the silver dragon shot white light into the golden dragon's eyes. The world went black as Garath sunk to the floor falling into a deep sleep.

"Then sleep well my young kin, you deserve a rest." The silver dragon turned his attention back to the

164

poisoned arrow. Tools and bottles of every mixture floated off the shelves to the table in front of him as he visually examined this new source of trouble.

Dram and Lo'Lith launched into the air as soon as they cleared the cave opening. Although he had a thousand questions for her, he would have to wait until she was ready to talk. *"You have been through a lot, let me flush out some game for you."* Lo'Lith too tired to argue agreed as she landed a short distance from the edge of the forest. Dram banked right and landed over a hundred yards downwind at the edge of the foliage. Running into the trees, he worked his way into a position in front of Lo'Lith. Letting out a loud roar, he charged his way back in her direction making as much noise as possible. Prey jumped out in every direction, once seeing Dram they ran towards open and the waiting dragon. Lo'Lith had crouched low in the rocks so she wouldn't be seen until the last second, rearing up she slashed at several deer that had left the safety of the forest. As Dram left the trees, he could see that she had killed enough for them both, letting the other game run back into the woods. Dragons only hunted for food not sport, there was no reason to kill more than they could eat.

Neither spoke as they ate, ripping into the soft venison, a rarity this high in the mountains. The forest was made by dragons thousands of years ago, everything from the dirt to the trees and animals for the members of the Council. There were no natural predators except for the dragons. Careful tending from the members of the Council kept the food source well stocked. Not only prey but also bountiful plants that fed his kind. The forest and its occupants did well, thriving from the ample water rising through the underground springs and the natural heat of the volcano itself. It was a sanctuary that few dragons had ever visited, though all of his kind was welcome. A place of meditation and insight, the ample food supply was meant to leave more time for conjecture and inner thought. Dram knew this area well for his father was the Speaker of the Council years ago. A life long gone, he remembered the days of playing in the lake, the teachings of the elders that few dragons got to experience. He was so prideful back then, thinking he knew more than any, even his teachers. He was going to bring his race back to the old ways single-handedly, great works of power and art once again created by his children. Too late, he saw the naivety of his plans, the lack of wisdom that still gave him nightmares to this day.

Both finished with their meal as Lo'Lith turned to Dram. "You still don't forgive yourself, do you?" More of a statement than a question, the black dragon shook his head no. "Me either, there isn't a day that goes by that I don't wish I could have traded places with her."

Anger ripped through Dram, not at Lo'Lith but it ended pointed at her for lack of other targets. "You were not responsible! You did not get my family killed!"

"They were my family too Dram and I forgive you." Without waiting for a reply, Lo'Lith launched into flight heading for the lake to wash off her meal. Dram's anger could not be quelled by one comment; it was anger at himself, for not being more. There were not any words that would bring his family back, no remarks that would ease the fact that he did not protect them.

Shame keeping him from talking more to Lo'Lith, Dram headed back to the cave to see how things were progressing. The Speaker was busy running experiments

166

on the arrow trying to find out what the poison was that nulled their magic. Garath was asleep where he had left him along with Danielle. Her breathing was steady showing signs of improvement.

"Any news of what we are dealing with? Can we fight this?" The Speaker ignored Dram's comment, still intent on his experiments to find out what the poison really was. Dram knew better than to upset the leader of the Council. Enlightened as they were they had little tolerance for those that challenged them. They led a life of meditation and solitude to help guide the dragons. They asked nothing in return, but that they are left alone until they are needed. Even then, they could only advise, there was no true leader of dragons. It was a thankless task they took up for the benefit of all, and it deserved his respect.

Lying on the floor next to Garath, Dram thought he would keep watch over Danielle. More tired than he thought he was soon asleep, this time the old nightmares did not come but new ones of poison arrows killing all those around him and powerless to stop any of it.

"Dram, wake up, we have work to do." The Speaker nudged the black dragon, trying to rouse him. "The Council has convened, we need you to tell us of your mission. The woman is awake and doing better but there is little she can tell us."

Dram blurry eyed followed the silver dragon through several tunnels before coming to the Council hall. Nine raised platforms lined the outer walls of the room; between each were the same glowing lights that lit the room where they removed the arrow from Danielle. Dram had been here before many times in the last twenty years. The Council of dragons was once again in session. Garath and Lo'Lith were already in the chamber. The black dragon walked up to his friends and waited for the Council to start.

"Dram, can you tell us of your mission and what you have learned over the last three weeks?" The Speaker was once again perched on the dais at the end of the room. Few of the Council ever spoke but for the Speaker. The Council communicates with each other in a form of mind speak far faster than normal, so it was favorable for only one of them to speak with others.

Dram told them of his trip to the capital and his experience with the mercenaries and Bowlsy. There was a long pause, as the Council contemplated what Dram had said about the army of supposed dragon slayers.

"Lo'Lith, I can't guess what you have been through, but can you tell us of your experience with being captured by these men?" The tone of the Speaker was far gentler, trying to bring the story out of the green dragon. Slowly at first then coming out in a rush, she told the Council of how she was captured, the experiments they did to her with the stuff the humans called dragon's bane. She stopped for a second looking at her right claw, the missing talon telling of the atrocities that the humans were willing to go to. No one said a word as she continued the story of the dismemberment and the battle before Dram showed up.

The Speaker conveyed with his brethren in mind speak, while the three dragons waited. "The situation is worse than I feared, this new dragon's bane is one thing, but the human's willingness to keep dragons alive for the sake of creating weapons is too appalling. I have analyzed the poison the best I can, it seems to react to our magic as a catalyst, turning our own powers against us. I still have more to learn about it, but one thing is clear, we have only one solution, we must go to war with this new threat and any humans that help them. The Council feels there is no other alternative or we all face annihilation. We take a stand now for all our kin." The Speaker's speech, although meant to be bold was filled with sadness.

"We will call a gathering for the spring; my brothers will head out to spread the word to our people. I urge you, do not take matters into your own hands. We will need a united front if we are to tackle this new menace. Dram, can you stay behind a minute?" At the hint from the Speaker, the rest of the dragons headed out of the room.

"Dram, the dragon's graveyard no longer protects us with this new threat. We have to even the odds against this dragon's bane. I need you to do something. It may sound like blasphemy, but it is our only solution. Will you to go to the dragon's graveyard and retrieve its power? It's a power different from our own and our only chance to counteract this poison"

Dram stood in disbelief at what the Speaker was asking. For thousands of years, the graveyard protected his kin from being used as weapons of power. "Won't that leave us more vulnerable than ever?"

"I don't believe so. Few know the ancient art of necromancy. Those that do I imagine are working for this new group if they are as well connected as you believe. If we don't stop this menace, graveyard or not they will destroy us all. We need every advantage we can get."

"No one knows the actual location for the graveyard, all I can tell you is that it is located in Mont Blanc. Do you know this place?"

There seemed to be no end of assault on Dram's grasp of reality. "Yes, but that is too high for any dragon to fly except by magic."

"Can you think of a safer place? The entrance to the graveyard is not going to be at the bottom of the mountain but more likely before the summit. Good luck Dram, I will look after your friends while you are gone."

Dram walked out of the Council chambers still in a daze by the events of the meeting. War, Dragon's Graveyard, dragon's bane, and a gathering, events were happening faster than he could truly comprehend. What impact would these have on the future or on his kin? Would there be any dragons, or for that matter, would there be any humans when all this was done. Caught up in his own thoughts as he walked, he almost ran into Garath bringing fresh water from the lake for Danielle.

"How is she?"

"Better, she was conscious earlier and told us what her brother was planning. Do you know he was at the battle of Greytock? That he saw the whole thing from up on the mountain?" Garath told him about her brother and that he was behind the plot on her family.

"I must go on another mission. If I am not back soon then I might not be back at all. Take care of your self and Danielle." Garath didn't say a word as Dram walked out to the front of the cave mouth. Shaking his head, the golden dragon headed back to the room where Danielle was resting. One day his friend would know peace he hoped.

Dram landed at the base of the mountain known as Mont Blanc or White Mountain for the snow that covered its

peak year around. It had been two days since he left the
home of the Council over fifty miles away. He could
have used his magic to help with the flight but something
in the back of his mind made him keep it in reserve.
Although that distance for a dragon in a single day is a
lot, the climb in altitude and thinner air the closer he got
to the mountain was very taxing.

Now he would have to find the entrance to the
graveyard. The range from the north looked like a
massive single peak rising up to challenge the sky itself.
From the south, two rows of jagged smaller peaks formed
their way down the side of the ridgeline forming a bowl
in between. At the bottom of the bowl, a large glacier
wound its way down the mountain to the lower hills.
Even with the unusually warm summer and then fall, the
mountain was still covered in snow. Circling more of the
base, Dram landed to rest and find some food. The night
was coming, and he still had not found a sign of an
entrance to the graveyard.

The next morning, the sun was out in full force, lighting
up the white peak like a giant diamond. The black dragon
decided to explore the glacier and bowl area. The
mountain air was too thin for flying without magic, so
Dram saved his power and crawled his way up the
flowing ice. The slope was slippery but smooth from the
summer's sun melting the ice daily only to refreeze at
night. Dram's claws kept easy purchase as he crawled his
way up to the start of the bowl of the mountain. He was
awed at the beauty and majesty of the site before him.
Rock spires like dragon's teeth lined each side of the
depression, almost like the bottom jaw of a dragon. Dram
kept crawling up the river of ice until he was in the center
of the bowl. Jagged peaks surrounded him on all sides

except for the direction of the glacier. If this was the home of the Dragon's Graveyard then no one since the time of Saris had been here, human or dragon.

The sun was almost at midday when Dram spied a flash off one of the rock cliffs. Ice had been melting all morning causing some reflections as the water trickled over the ancient glacier, ready for another trick of the light, Dram moved across the frozen river for a better look.

Now close to the rock face, he tried to find the flash he had seen from the center of the bowl. Jagged peaks towered almost a thousand feet above his head. The curvature of the slope itself hid his view of the area he had seen before. Resigning himself to no other alternative, he started climbing the rocky cliff face.

Several hundred feet above the glacier Dram was still trying to find the area he had glimpsed from down below. The climb was not actually dangerous. If he slipped, he could float down and start over again. The air was too thin this high up to fly but he could glide easily enough if he had to. The climb back up was what he wanted to avoid.

Clearing the last outcropping, Dram finally sat on a ledge almost to the top of the jagged ridgeline. Two silver statues of dragons stood at each side of a cave mouth just big enough for a dragon to walk into. The ledge was unusually warm even with the autumn sun shining directly on it. Dram surveyed the horizon taking in the breathtaking beauty before him. He could almost see the home of the Council more than fifty miles to the south. Turning his attention to the statues, they seemed more like sentries more than the decorative sculptures they appeared.

Using his inner sight, he could not sense anything magical about the statues or the mouth of the cave itself. Seeing no reason to stall, he started to walk between the stone guardians into the cave.

Silver light flashed from the two statues, surrounding Dram in a sphere of energy. Unable to move, Dram struggled to free himself but to no avail. Bringing his own magic to bare he tried to rip a hole in the magical energy, but it only shot back at himself, burning him. The Sphere kept getting tighter and tighter until he could no longer breath, hard enough as it was in this thin atmosphere. Blackness took over as the last of his breath was pushed out of his lungs from the crushing energy.

The soft tap of claws on hard stone echoed across the room as Lo'Lith entered the chamber where Danielle slept as a crackling fire near the far wall was the only light in the room. Danielle laid on a crude bed of furs and straw, making small moans of pain both mental and physical, in her sleep.

"Are you awake?" the green dragon said softly. The furs pulled aside as Danielle tried to shake off a drowsy fog.

"Kind of, it's hard to sleep with all this pain." Peering into the dark she could just make out the color of the dragon's form. "You are the dragon from the courtyard," she said as a statement, not a question.

"Yes, I wanted to thank you for saving my life. I heard your conversation up on the balcony. You gave up so much, why, he was your brother and you don't even know me?" Once she started the works seem to stumble out of Lo'Lith all at once.

"Please, come over by the fire so I can see you better."
As the green dragon hesitated, Danielle reassured her.
"It's all right, please I have lots of questions for you
also."

Lo'Lith carefully moved to the fireside of the bed, the
flames reflected off her emerald green skin. As the
dragon settled down on the warm cave floor, Danielle
started in on her questions, holding nothing back.

"Did you really kill my father?"

A mixed look of pain and anger shot back at the
wounded woman. Nothing was said for a minute until
Lo'Lith looked down from Danielle's resolute face and to
the large bandage still red from the seepage the night
before. Finally lowering her head to stare at the floor she
spoke.

"I killed many men that day. I have no idea which one
may have been your father. My only concern was an
escape, but in the end, they had me well trapped."

"It seems we both have been put into traps by my
brother. He was the one responsible for the deaths of both
my father and my uncle. You were just used like we all
were." Danielle's words seemed to take some of the
anger out of the dragon's expression, but the pain was
clearly still there.

"I thank you for your help in the courtyard, I really do
but I am scared for all the others of my race that will be
or have been subjected to that same fate by humans." The
last word the dragon spat out with contempt.

Trying to change the subject Danielle said, "Lo'Lith, did
you know about Garath and Dram rescuing me and our
trip together back to the capital?"

The green dragon took a second to grasp the change in conversation. "Yes, which is even more puzzling than ever. We have never given into the humans before."

Danielle thought for a moment before she started her next words. "Lo'Lith, I know our people have warred for years, but nothing Garath or Dram talked to me about had anything to do with one side surrendering to the other."

Lo'Lith raised her head a little at the words started to sink in. Danielle continued, "our people have a lot of misunderstandings about each other. Most of my people don't even know dragons exist. They think you are fairytales told to frighten children to be good. Besides the farmers near the mountains that come up missing a cow or sheep now and then, none of them even really care if you are real and live hundreds of miles away. Honestly, our farmers have more problems with wolves and mountain cats than we do with dragons."

The green dragon was skeptical about Danielle's argument. People have always hated dragons, from the dawn of time. Why would it change now? But there was a spark of hope in what the woman said, something that Lo'Lith really needed to be able to believe in. She slowly nodded understanding and for her to continue.

Danielle, sensing she might be too optimistic didn't want to sugarcoat the reality of it. "Don't think my brother is not dangerous, he is and has a lot of resources. It's not going to be easy but it's not hopeless. I have contacts also and he is a small part of a very large world."

The dragon let the words swim around in her mind, there were so many years of history that she could not forget. On the other claw, here was a human that risked her life, against her own brother to save hers. "I will think heavily on what you have said."

"Good," then with a mischievous smile partially wincing from the pain, she said. "So, what can you tell me about Garath…..?"

Dram crouched on a barren plain. Gone were the two statues standing in front of him just a minute before. As far as he could see the land was nothing but gray, even the grass he stood on was a dull charcoal, that showed no variation in color. In his four hundred years, he had never seen a world like this, blades of grass seemed to blend into the ground leaving no hint of dirt, and the sky was the same color as the rest of the land. Dram took his claw and grabbed at the ground, he could feel resistance, then something gave, but nothing came up in his hand.

"Where am I?" Dram shouted. The question was rhetorical, but something answered anyway.

"You are here." Spinning his head around Dram strained to see in all directions at once. There was still nothing but the dull gray of before.

"Where is here, who are you?"

In front of Dram, a silvery colored light appeared. Like a crack in the world, it seemed not to be part of this reality, even though the world he was in didn't seem to be real. Slowly the light grew larger until it was the size of Dram himself. Without seeming to change the light turned into the shape of a platinum dragon. The body was in the prime of youth but the eyes, ancient even to a dragon's standard, stared not at Dram but at his soul.

"Still asking questions to what you already know the answers to? Has it been so long since you have thought for yourself? Letting the Council run you like a puppet into a grandstand of madness?"

The voice came from everywhere at once, running through Dram's mind like an ocean flowing over a grain of sand. If there had been a million dragons on that plain each would have heard it exactly the same way, felt it exactly the same way.

"Saris," was all Dram could say. All dragons knew the story of the platinum dragon. He was the closest thing dragons had to a god. When Magi were using the parts of dragons to augment their own power Saris made the

Dragon's Graveyard so that no further exploitation could be made of a dead dragon. He was a power beyond even the comprehension of a people who lived thousands of years. In the end, it is said that he sacrificed himself for it.

"No, no. You're not in Saris. Nice place though, a little more colorful than this."

"No, you're Saris. Did you bring me here?" Dram had completely lost his control in the situation.

"Hey! Don't be calling names here. I try to help a fellow dragon out and I get bit in the tail." The radiant dragon lost his mirth and his tone became serious. "As for your question, yes and no."

"What do you mean?" Dram was getting a little annoyed with the roundabout answers he was getting, even if this was Saris.

"You've always been here. I just showed you what it looked like. What a mess."

Dram was losing all patience with this one. Platinum Dragon or not he was going to get some answers. The dragon then looked at Dram and said one word. "Think."

His mind raced as he tried to comprehend the dragons meaning. Then a quick flash of lightning lit the sky and Dram had the answer. "I'm in my mind."

"Well now, you're not as slow-witted as you first started out." Dram cringed at the remark but at least he had an answer. The dragon could deal a little better with the situation.

The voice became very serious. "Dram the path you take will have more ramifications than you will ever know. It will be a necessary travel, and at the end, you will finally know of what I speak. However, to survive the journey you will have to battle your own demons. They will only

179

cripple you in the coming battle. Remember, at the light, you will find yourself." Then the dragon slowly started to fade away.

"Wait there's more I want to ask," But Dram's plea had no impact. Slowly the light vanished leaving the place somehow lonelier than before. The words kept ringing in his head. "At the light, you will find yourself." Only the words seemed to run together into a rhyme of nonsense.

Dram searched the horizon for any sign of landmarks. In all directions, the barren land seemed to go on forever. Only a thin line distinguished sky from earth. If this was his mind, then even that was not real. Like a false dawn, the grayness seemed to lighten in one direction. Seeing nothing better Dram leaped into flight. Muscles tightened as powerful legs tore from the ground, wings snapped out and down pulling the large body up into the air. Repeatedly the wings flapped to speed the dragon along. Once high enough he stretched out his wings to glide on the air currents, saving his strength.

Even from this altitude, the land did not seem to change, the flat gray plains extending on forever. Dram then used his magic to speed himself along. Willing the molecules in his body to accelerate in the direction he wanted regardless of wind or wing. Soft orange bits of lightning caressed his body showing the kind of magic in use. Caution kept him from using his whole power, not knowing what lay ahead; he may have to save something in case of the unexpected.

Suddenly the flat grassland stopped, turning into a giant mountain range. Jagged peaks rivaled the sky, making a barrier that ran in both directions forever. The faint glow Dram had seen earlier seemed to be brighter coming from the other side of the impossibly massive wall.

Dram studied the range with the experience of one born to the high ledges of the mountains. These weren't like any he'd ever seen before. They were more akin to giant crystal spires or a line of sharp teeth to keep out all that would dare to enter. Higher and higher, he tried to climb but the peaks rose to touch the heavens themselves. Hours of struggle led to no avail. Tired and distraught Dram tried to land.

As soon as Dram touched down, the small ledge gave way, sending bits of stone and dirt sliding down the nearly vertical slope. The rocks turned into an avalanche taking out more ledges below. Using daggered talons Dram dug into the cliff face, into a stone that no dragon had ever touched before.

"What kind of world is this?" Dram swore. The rock moved like a living being. Claws that first clasped solid rock seemed to clasp air a second later. Time and again, he grabbed the rock but just as the mountain fought him from going over it, it fought him from resting.

Dram brought his magic to bear on the rock. Focusing his mind on the earth around him he tried by force of will to stabilize the ground around himself. Slowly the rock hardened making a ledge for him to rest on. Concentrating Dram tried to push his control to more of the mountain. If he could control this little bit of ground, then maybe he would have some control with the rest. Using his senses Dram tried to see into the heart of the mountain itself. Visions slammed back at him from all sides making him almost lose control of the ledge he was on. Anger, despair, and sorrow filled his mind with hopelessness. Dram reeled from the mental onslaught. Then fire fought fire as Drams anger clashed with that of the visions. Will battled will to a stalemate neither side could win, and the mountain was growing bigger.

Dram pushed himself to the limits of his endurance, then beyond what he could control. Something broke, some little light in the back of his mind pierced through the blackness. Understanding fought anger now. Instead of fire feeding fire, it was as if water dowsed the flames that were burning his soul. Slowly the mountain turned to mud, then to water, washing Dram away in a sea of emotions. Feelings buried long ago were once again coming to the surface, letting him deal with them in a different light, a different frame of mind. The pain of the past knocked Dram to his knees. Memories long forgotten surfaced, no longer suppressed. The light pulsed from ahead, turning the once dark mud to a crystal gray. Then slowly the waters receded as Dram realized they were his own tears, leaving the barren plain once again in all directions. This time the light showed a bit brighter, a bit less repressive.

Dram viewed the horizon once more. The light was again in one direction leaving a clear trail for which to follow. Dram leaped into the air. Still, he was astonished at the way the ground acted. Nothing moved, no grass blowing from the power of his wings, no dust, not even torn earth from his talons ripping the ground. Then his thoughts turning to more important issues, used his magic to propel him faster than he had ever gone before. Power didn't seem to make a difference in this world so saving it wouldn't help him in the end. The wind increased as his speed exceeded all physical limits.

As if a mountain struck him, the wind slammed him to the earth. Hurricane-like gales bashed him as he tried to make his way forward. Crawling was all he could do as funnels of air and water crashed on him from above forcing him to the ground. Fighting the challenging wind was taking its toll. Fatigue set in as he used all his strength to keep crawling towards the light. Even the clear eyelids offered no protection for Dram's eyes as the hail and rain pelted his head like small rocks.

The storm, seeing that Dram was not going to be swayed, suddenly stopped. Clouds of wind and vapor came together forming into a giant version of Dram himself. A black dragon over one hundred feet high stood now before Dram. Black obsidian talons over half the length of his own body flexed, daring him to keep going. The giant dragon's eyes were of purest night, sucking in all the light around them. As the new dragon stepped towards Dram, the ground shook, causing him to lose his footing.

Reflexes took over. This was something that Dram could handle. A real enemy, even if it was himself. Launching into the air, he roared a challenge to the behemoth. Renewed strength flowed in his tired muscles as Dram soared to take on the new dragon. Reaching head height dram halted, staring at his enemy in the eyes.

"Your will, not pass!" boomed the obsidian giant. Black acid dripped off twenty-foot fangs burning holes in the ground below. Dram was not here to talk. Taking the small pause, he attacked. Flying in between the larger dragon's arms, Dram unleashed his own breath weapon at the creature's face. The behemoth's head was as large as Dram himself. Hot acid shot out of his mouth frying the eyes of his enemy. Flying past the great head, Dram grabbed hold of the long horns at the back of the skull. Holding tight he sunk his teeth into the tough skin of the new dragon's neck. Roaring from the pain, the behemoth turned to grab Dram with his right claw. Moving to the

183

center of the neck, he strained to stay out of the giants reach. Sinking his teeth once again into the back of the neck, Dram tried to do as much damage as possible. Suddenly a huge snap stunned him as the behemoth's tail whipped him from behind almost ripping his teeth out of his mouth. The action had knocked Dram far enough to the side that the Giant dragon could grasp the smaller attacker. The massive claw wrapped around the smaller dragon's chest. An agonizing cry escaped from Dram as the pressure started to crush him. The large dragon freeing the nuisance from the back of his neck flung him at the ground. Dram had never felt such pain before as it seemed every bone in his body would break. Lying on the ground Dram gave a brief thought about giving up. The odds were just too great, the sacrifices too much. Straining with every fiber of his being, Dram tried to see what the other dragon was doing.

The behemoth was just standing there watching with those cold black eyes, peering into Dram's soul. Forcing himself to his feet Dram realized that he was in one piece. Although sore as hell, not a bone was broken.

"Your will, not pass!" boomed the giant dragon again.

"Why?" Dram shouted back. His voice seemed so weak compared to that of the other dragon. The bigger dragon said nothing in return.

"Why do you keep me from that which I must do!" shouted Dram again.

"Because you must!" he boomed again.

Tired, sore and completely at a loss, Dram could not see any way to win. If he tried to out fly the creature it would only catch him in his tired condition. Obviously, he could not do much damage to him, not without being obliterated himself. While Dram contemplated his options, the giant dragon just sat there and watched with cold dark eyes.

Feeling his strength return Dram tried once more, this time to get past his enemy. Launching himself to the left, he used the last of his magic to fly past the hulking figure. Every ounce of speed he had he put into staying just out of the other dragons reach. Yet another giant claw snatched Dram out of the air and hurled him back to earth. This time the ground was not so lenient. Bones snapped leaving Dram in a pile on the grey carpet like grass. Not being able to move Dram could barely see the new dragon in the same spot he had been the whole time. Anger washed over him at being so helpless. There was no fear, no sorrow just the madness of being so easily overcome. Sanity slipped as the red hate, not at the enemy before him but at himself for being so weak, took over his mind. Dram let the madness consume him. Too long, had he fought the world, fought himself and won neither. In the madness, there was no fighting, just the comforting peace that Dram so longed.

Once again, madness brought clarity to his mind. He hated himself for so long because he was weak because he could not save his family and now he might not save his race. The madness swept away the emotions that clouded his view. As the self hate that he had held all those years slipped away, so did the size of the giant dragon before him. Dram was not god, yet he held himself to standards only a perfect being could keep, to blame only a god could handle. The madness took away the guilt, the hate and left only the truth. That none of this was Dram's fault, that nothing he could have done or can do now will ever change the past. He could not be responsible for the actions of others. That he could not prepare for every possibility.

As the guilt subsided so did the dragon in front of him, he realized what the mammoth version of himself was saying, "Your Will, Not Pass!" Not, "You Will Not Pass." Again, he was fighting his own reluctance to move forward. Now the same size as Dram himself the once giant dragon was still shrinking. The clarity, centered inside his madness, started to grow. It pushed out the madness, healing body and mind while cleansing his spirit. New strength flowed as bones mended and ligaments healed anew. The dragon in front of him was only knee high. Without a second thought, Dram launched into flight, heading once more to the white light. The previously mighty dragon below him could do nothing now to stop him, its power taken away forever.

Now Dram was racing again towards the now bright light. The ground below him had taken on a light silver color, gone was the charcoal grey that he started with. With ever more speed, he tried to move closer to the far-off light.

What seemed like hours left Dram no closer to his target than after his last battle. The distance was hard to judge in this grey expanse, but he was sure that he was not gaining ground. Landing on the soft grasslands, he surveyed the entire horizon. The light was clearly in one direction, although the color of the land was almost white. After each battle, the shade lightened a bit leaving the featureless landscape less gloomy than before.

There was something bugging Dram since his last battle. He understood that somehow, he was in his mind and that the battles he fought were against himself. He also was not sure if fighting was the answer or not. Even though he did not win, the battle led to understanding. Without that he doubted that he would see things so clear now. There must be something different from this test since nothing seemed to be opposing him.

Concentrating on everything that had happened since he started this journey of the mind, Dram ran over every step. Something the giant dragon had said when he asked why he would not let him pass. "Cause you must!" ran repeatedly in Drams mind. There had to be some deeper meaning to what the behemoth said. Of course, he must, he had to. The only way out was at the light, according to Saris. He must get to the light, he must save his people and he must deal with one more issue. The thing he had hidden away for so long from himself. Why must he deal with that? Why must he?

This time without the madness, Dram realized what he must do. Ever since Greytock, he had been reactive to the events that surrounded his life. Like a wild animal running in fear, it will do what it must to live, never taking the initiative to solve the source of that fear. There is a big difference between having to do something and really wanting to do it. No amount of duty, threats or even self-preservation could make Dram do what he needed. He had to want it of his own accord, be ready for it and willing to endure to see the end. No amount of coercion could set him on that path.

Dram turned and faced the light on the horizon. He knew now what he faced and what the light really was. He was no longer running but willing and wanting to face that which he had suppressed all these years. It was time to end this.

"I am ready now!" Dram shouted at the light. Like a shooting star, the light grew as it hurled towards Dram. Not a muscle twitched as he waited for the growing white

187

glow to come to him. As it came closer, Dram could feel the last boundaries he had placed on himself dissolve to nothing. Twenty years of self-repression flowed away leaving no barrier for the incoming light. Faster the light accelerated the closer it moved to Dram. Faster than any arrow, it slammed into his chest, knocking him to the ground. The light infused him, becoming one with every cell of his body. The end had finally begun.

CHAPTER 12

The fires in the hatchery were burning high, keeping the room warmer than a hot summer's day. Twelve braziers in all lined the stone walls of the round room. Sixty-eight eggs completely covered the hot sand filled floor. Only a stone path, a dragon's width, ran between the braziers and the eggs allowing the fires to be refueled. Dram stood in the doorway between the hatchery and the storage room where the wood and coal were kept for heating. Smiling with pride, he watched what would become his first children, the first of many children with his beloved.

The tap of claws on stone turned him to see his mate Andrinin. She always took his breath away, but now she glowed from motherhood that warmed Dram more than the nearby fires. Andrinin had the skin of the lightest blue sapphire that glowed even in the depths of night. Dram would lay awake for hours just to watch her sleep. The blue was almost like lightning as it seemed to dance along with her body from the deep breathing of slumber.

"Ever watchful my love?" Andrinin moved next to her lifemate to see her first batch of eggs. The lights from the fires reflected off her mate's golden skin sending sparkles of glitter across the ceiling. She was so proud of her mate. There was something different about him that she had spotted right away. Andrinin remembered when she had first seen him soaring high above the small mountain lake where she was bathing. He was crimson then, full of fire and passion. As handsome and large as any dragon that ever tried for her affections, he was the only one that never chased her. Some dragons had no interest in families or mates. They sought other pursuits, power, greed even things that most dragons dared not to talk. She knew that this was not what Dram was about. On a chance, she was the one that chased him. Well, it was not much of a chase once she found out for all his fire and passion, he was just shy. Of course, she was not going to let something like that keep her from what she wanted. All the cocky, arrogant and overzealous courtiers that vied for her attention couldn't hold a dragon's breath to the caring that Dram had shown her over the years. That was over fifty years ago, and she only loved him more with every day.

"They are beautiful. I could not have imagined I would feel this way." The excitement ran through Dram like fire. Nothing could top the way he felt. He was so proud of his mate and himself. It was not the number of eggs, although it was a large batch. It was the beginning of an adventure they were setting on, one that would be new in the evolution of all dragons. A great number of his kind was not concerned with teaching their young. The genetic knowledge left most with all they needed to know to start life. Anything more was left to each dragon to learn on his own. Dram had the idea that teaching his children would bring a new era to his people. He felt his race was regressing from the lack of challenge in their education.

"Let's take a moment for ourselves, the sun is warm outside, the currents will be strong through the mountains." Andrinin had been cooped up for a month in the hatchery. Three weeks it took to lay all the eggs, now a week later she had cabin fever. "Come, my love, let us take a break, our children are safe, the fires will be warm for hours. We can touch our wings again as we used too." With an offer like that, how could Dram refuse? One last glance at his offspring, he closed the doors to the hatchery to keep the heat in. If the temperature dropped on the eggs to below a warm day, they may not hatch. Not every egg in a hatching cracked but he would see that they got the best chance possible.

Beating Andrinin to the ledge Dram launched into the canyon upside down so he could see his mate as he descended into the valley below. Wings outstretched in a crucified position, he fell, waiting for his mate to join him. Andrinin launched mirroring his position. Her decent reached his as they grasped each other. The fall was short since the hatchery was low in altitude compared to the massive mating heights of the Alps. However, they were not mating but enjoying one another's company. The lake rushed up as they held out before disengaging. Each smiled at the other as they stared eye to eye before the release. Wings snapped as they pushed off one another, narrowly missing the water, the wind from their bodies causing ripples across the still blue surface.

They worked their way up on the warm spring drafts. Flying together with years of precision, wings barely touching, they made their approach to the highest peaks. The sun was high overhead, heating the rocky ledges as Dram landed on one of the highest. The ledge was more than large enough for both of them, overlooking the valleys far below. After Dram retracted his wings and moved to the side Andrinin came to land next to him, playfully tackling him as she did. Losing the battle Dram fell to his side letting his mate lay across his chest. She nuzzled his neck with the side of her head, lightly scratching the tough hide. It was not long wrapped in each other's arms that both fell asleep, the waning sun the only audience for their slumber.

The cold chill of shadow woke Dram as the sun started to set over the horizon. "Andrinin, we slept too long." Slowly she came awake as weeks of nearly no sleep was somewhat caught up. "It's ok my love, there was plenty of fuel on the fires. They will still be going when we get back." Slowly untangling herself from Dram's grasp, she stood on the ledge overlooking the waning sun. It would be dark she thought before they got back home. The hatchery had to be kept low in altitude or the thin air would dissipate the heat too fast at night, possibly retarding some of the eggs.

Without another word, Andrinin launched off the ledge with Dram close behind. Darkness came fast as not only the sun lowered on the horizon, but the shadows filled the mountain valleys as they blocked its rays as well. Dram was first into the gorge where they had located their hatchery. Most dragons never built their own hatcheries any more. Willing to use ones filled with the dust of ages. Dram and Andrinin wanted more for their offspring. Part of the reason they waited so long before deciding to nest. Young dragons are on their own as soon as they can fly. Once the last of the hatchlings take flight, the parent dragons hopefully clean the area for the next expectant parents and move on themselves. Lineage and teaching the young was not too important to his race. Something Dram hoped to change. He and his mate both being seekers of knowledge wanted to pass that heritage on to their children if they wanted it. In his mind, Dram could picture his offspring playing in the lake below, running up the trail that led back to the hatchery and gliding back down. He saw the fires of the main room burning as he and his mate taught their children the wonders of the world. The things that his races genetic memory would not pass on, not with much detail, things dragons had forgotten, thinking unimportant in their long existence.

Dram landed on the ledge outside the lair. Like cold daggers down his spine, his senses were set on edge. Something was wrong, very wrong. The smell of man was all about. Leaping forward he raced for the hatchery, his mate close behind. The door was slightly ajar as Dram approached and stopped before it. Dread filled the pit of his being as he dared to open it. The sound of Andrinin coming up next to him gave him the courage to enter the next room. The lights of the braziers still lit the hatchery, blinding Dram as he first entered. As his eyes adjusted, the horror was worse than he could have ever imagined.

Broken shells and unborn embryos covered the sticky sand. Not one egg had been left intact from the slaughter. Andrinin rushed past Dram to search the crushed remains of her babies. She only confirmed what he already knew, all their children were dead. All he could do was stare as the pain racked his body to the point that his muscles would not work. His mate looked at him now, pleading in her eyes. Bits of shell, sand and unborn fluid stuck to her arms and claws. She then looked down at her hands, stained with the blood of her offspring. The scene turned Dram's pain to rage, fire burned through his mind now. Heading back outside Dram stopped at the ledge. Filling his lungs as full of air as he could, he let go the rage call. A scream more than a roar, the sounds carried for miles. Magnified by pain and carried by emotion, the rage call would be heard by dragons for miles. Dram would hunt down those that did this, making them pay for their treachery.

Launching off the ledge he headed to the opening of the valley where the river exited from the lake. It was the only way that humans could enter or leave the area. The sheer cliff walls were too steep for any to climb. Even the water came in from a hundred-foot waterfall near the upper end of the lake.

Nearing the mouth of the valley Dram used his inner

sight to look for his attackers. Only a few small animals showed up in his enhanced vision. Knowing the attackers could not be too far ahead Dram elevated to a higher position to see more of the forest extending to the southwest. From this height, it was harder to distinguish individual shapes, but he should be able to see a large party. Only the small glow of the local wildlife could be spotted. He could track them in the dark but would be a slow process, turning around he headed back to see who answered the rage call.

Garath sat on the ledge to the hatchery as Dram returned. By his face, Dram could tell that Andrinin had already told him the whole story. Several more dragons, some Dram did not recognize circled overhead. As he landed next to Garath, a slight nod was all it took to let him realize that Garath was there for whatever was needed. Heading into the hatchery, he found Andrinin with her mother Lo'Lith in the doorway. His mate was still shaking, although cleaner than when she left. She turned to look at Dram pleading in her eyes. Bowing his head to hers, he whispered in her ear. "I will make this right." The shakes stopped as Drams words hit her. A slight nod and Dram headed back to the ledge.

"We fly!" the roar echoed off the canyon walls almost as loud as the rage call itself. "Humans will see what power they have unleashed today!" All followed as Dram dove off the ledge heading to where river exited the valley. Here they would find the tracks that would lead them to revenge and justice.

Landing in an open area near the water, Dram searched for any signs that would give him a direction. Not even the smell of humans could be detected. Calling to Garath to search the other side of the stream he told the others to circle above him. The humans may have used the river to hide their smell for a way, but they could not stay in the water indefinitely. Within a mile another waterfall, though small, was too much for horses or man to go over.

Dram motioned for Garath to follow on the other side of the bank as they worked their way down the river. It was three hours past dark, if they were able to find the trail before dawn they should be able to catch them before they got too far. Humans cannot move very fast at night, but in the morning could get a huge lead. Garath, farther along the stream came up with something. The smell of horse and tracks were leading away out of the water to the south. Using his mind Dram let Andrinin know to head south with the group above. Normally mind speech would never travel that far without the closeness between him and his mate. The circling dragons all started to head south while Dram and Garath stayed on the ground following the trail. If the path changed direction or the flying dragons spotted something they would let each other know.

They followed the smell through the high grass in the darkness of the new moon. Tracks would not be seen until first light, the sent of horses was all they had till then. Suddenly the trail stopped. With his sight, Dram could make out the grass in the open field where the horse sent disappeared. The grass was leaning back towards the river again. The men had doubled back. Dram roared out of rage, the ground reverberated with his frustration. *Back to the river,* he told his mate as he and Garath launched into a short flight. Reaching the river, Dram and Garath took up their search of each bank again. The waterfall was still a way off when they found another smell leading away from the river. Not to be misled again

Dram asked one of the flying dragons to track the trail on the ground while he and Garath continued along the river.

Nearly to the waterfall, Dram received word from Andrinin. The other trail was false also. They had found a riderless horse a few miles to the south. It was just another ruse to keep them off the trail. Dram was past fury now, the cold that ran through his blood showed no emotion. Steadily he and Garath kept working their way to the waterfall.

Just as he had expected strong smells led from both sides of the river right before where the water fell over the edge of the jagged riverbed. Neither trail led back to the river. *Garath and the others follow the south trail, Andrinin, Lo'Lith and I will take the north one. I have a feeling that both trails will be real.* Andrinin repeated Drams words as Garath followed the southern trail. Time was running out. The false trails had taken up valuable time and it was only an hour until dawn.

Hurrying Dram did not care if he overran the trail or not. The tracks he followed were visible and had many scents, one of which was definitely man. He did not want to recall Garath since it could be that the party may have split up. *You two scout ahead, maybe you can spot them faster than following the trail.* The dragon told his two companions. With their night sight, they should be able to see anyone for miles if they were still in the area. The trail seemed to head steadily to the Southwest. Dram figured they had following it too long to be a fake. It worried him that the trail was so straight. It meant that whoever he was pursuing was racing to safety. If they did not catch them soon they might have a larger problem on their hands.

Garath and the others are returning, Andrinin warned

197

Dram. That meant the other trail was also another decoy. Doubling his speed, he figured that there would be no more detours. The rest of this group was heading somewhere fast, so would he.

The sun was just coming over the mountains to the east as the dragons crested the last ridge before what his people called Greytock. The trail they followed led straight to a valley where the only human castle in the area stood. The hovering dragons all landed next to Dram. The game had just changed for this was where the humans had gone and why they were in such a hurry to get there. Greytock was more than just a castle but a fortress used mainly in ancient times. Built to hold back the barbarian invaders from the north, it was designed to defend against any attack. From where he stood, Dram could make out that the battlements of Greytock filled with men. The humans were waiting for them. The whole event was evidently all planned.

"This is where you can turn back if you want, it's my fight, I will take my revenge." The tone in Dram's voice was cold, the other dragons could feel the hate in it.

"No Dram, this is all our fight. What they did is an affront to all dragon kind. They brought war to our children. I for one will pay with my life to see it never happens again." Dram was moved at Garath's reply. They had been close friends for years yet there was something more here. Dragons rarely ever put their lives in danger for one another, being individualistic and self-absorbed.

"Thank you, my friend, but I can't let Garath speak for you all. Anyone else want to leave?" As Dram looked from dragon to dragon, he saw the same determination that was in Garath's eyes. Nodding to them all, Dram turned once more to face the fortress across the valley.

"They are ready for us, this is not going to be easy. Garath and I will each take a team and hit the castle from opposite sides. On our approach, make it look like we are attacking straight on from this direction. As soon as you are in bow range Garath's team bank right while mine will go left. As soon as you reach the back of the castle, attack the back corner of your side. This should leave a good portion of their force at the front and able us to take out most of their number as they try to move to the back to engage us." It was a dangerous plan, gone was the feeling of self-preservation from his mind. This was revenge, fueled by hatred and loss and nothing would stop him. Dram divided the group of dragons into the two teams, each having fire, lightning, acid, and cold to round them out. A few minutes later everyone was ready.

"Now, let none live in that place after we are done!" Dram launched off the hillside with the others following him. Keeping his eyes focused on the battlements of the castle, he could feel Garath at his side.

Prepare for battle, as Dram spoke a soft glow surrounded all the dragons. Soft leathery skin turned to hardened scales, starting at the back of Dram's neck then moving down and across the back and legs. All thirteen dragons had hardened scale armor running the length of their bodies. Covering everywhere except wings and leg joints, where they could bind and inhibit agility. Dragon scales made a great armor, however, was heavy and impeded flying so were only used for battle. Dram looked to his right to see Garath fully decked out and ready for battle.

As they neared bow range, he could see the men on the battlements, bows in hand ready to fire. Dram told the others to split as the first volley was released from the ramparts. The arrows narrowly missed the two groups as they each headed for their side of the castle.

Garath banked to the right. *Stay Close, when I give the command to attach I want you to spread out to a dragon's breath of each other and hit those guards on the wall.* Garath wanted to widen out their field of attack as wide as possible.

The fortress was laid out in a square pattern with the main building in the center. The outer walls left roughly fifty yards of open ground to the keep. As Garath banked again heading to the rear wall he caught a glimpse inside. The entire marshaling yard was filled with men and war machines.

It's more of a trap than we thought. We need to break in at that corner and hold our position. Then we will need to fight our way to Dram's team from there. Their plan was to flank the main force with both groups coming from each side at the weakest point in their defenses. As the main human force split to come around the large building, they could pick them off before they could get set back up.

The men on the walls could be seen racing down the ramparts to keep the dragons in range but the speed of the dragons quickly outdistanced them. As the groups reached the back corner of the wall, Garath quickly accessed the situation. The twenty-foot-high wall was roughly ten feet wide at the top with a five-foot-high parapet running on the outside. Arrow slits ran every five feet or so through the upper railing, ending at a guard tower in the corner. Every hundred feet there was a small guard shack just big enough to block movement down the wall if the doors were barred from the inside. The idea was if the wall got breached the invaders couldn't access

the rest of the wall or get down to the courtyard below
without jumping.

NOW! The dragons moved as one unit as they attached
the wall. The handful of men stationed at the back of the
fortress were no match for the fire and lightning breath of
the five attackers. Garath, not liking things in his way
landed next to the guard tower, ripped it from the
foundation, sending it over the edge.

All the dragons were now perched on the wall, clearing
the ground below. To jump down now would risk being
impaled on the long spears carried by the soldiers.
Screams and curses came from the men below as they
tried to hold their ground until reinforcements would
arrive from the front of the keep.

*We don't have long before reinforcements, follow me in
one at a time.* With another spout of fire, Garath jumped
down to the dirt below, the area already cleared to
blackened charcoal. The remaining twenty men had
formed up a shield wall, lances protruding through the
gaps. The gold dragon blasted them with another round of
fire, but the wall held. Between the shields and the
padded armor, Garath could only irritate them and he was
already running out of fire. He would have to switch to
magic soon.

A white flash struck the middle of the group of men
sending several flying in all directions. The blue dragon
had just dropped down next to Garath and was opening
his mouth for another lightning attack. The men broke,
with the rest of the dragons now off the wall, the skirmish
was over.

Without warning the red dragon to Garaths left went
flying back and slammed into the wall. Protruding from
his chest was a wooden shaft the size of a small tree.

Garath stood stunned for a few seconds at the sheer power of what he just saw. Getting focused, he rallied the rest of the dragons.

Attack, we are sitting prey if we stay in one spot. The soldiers had stopped their retreat and had regrouped with the main force from the front of the keep. Horses were pulling what looked like a giant crossbow the size of a wagon. Two more were coming up after that still loaded with the large lances that had hit the red dragon just moments before.

Take out those machines, don't worry about the men. Garath said as he rushed the wall of soldiers protecting the large weapons. Moments before reaching the long pikes ready to impale his charge, Garath suddenly stopped and swung his large tale around and hit the men from the side. The first three soldiers flew into the rest taking down their defenses in one sweep. Leaping over the fallen bodies, he charged the unprepared soldiers, driving his way forward until he was within range of the three machines. Using his fire, he set everything ablaze within twenty feet of the large crossbows. The heavy bowstrings made a loud snap as it burned in two, the wood splintered from the intense heat then burst into flames. The second wagon exploded into a shower of debris as lightning from the blue dragon hit its mark.

The soldiers, seeing their weapons destroyed doubled their resolve. Lances formed to the front over shields held in formation. They wouldn't be so easily tricked again with a tail swipe. Garath had used too much fire and magic trying to destroy the war machines, keeping up his battle armor against the swords and lances of the soldiers was taking its toll. Now arrows were raining down from the archers on top of the wall. Their range was a lot farther than Garath's breath weapon.

A second red dragon moved in front of Garath. Arrows and long purple cuts covered his body. "Move back I will hold them off!" roared the red. Garath shot another burst of flame into the lancers. Nodding to the dragon, turned with the blue dragon and raced to the cover of the back of the keep. Battle rage could be heard behind them as the red dragon brought magic and fire to take on his attackers. Claw met shield then gave away to armor then flesh, spears met scale finally penetrating to the muscle underneath. As promised he kept the soldiers at bay while the other dragons regrouped. One final roar then nothing, the dragon's graveyard took another into its midst.

The white dragon still held the wall, keeping them from being outflanked. With his cold breath, he froze the guard shack, keeping the soldiers from coming down the top of the walkway. That did not keep the archers from firing from the other side. The arrows were starting to sting as the dragon's magic was starting to wane.

Move to behind the keep, we will regroup there and push to where the others are. Hopefully, they are doing better than we are. The white dragon leaped down from the wall and glided to where Garath and the blue dragon were behind the building. The soldiers were cautiously moving forward, without the archers and war machines it would be a sword to claw fight. Keeping the ranks tight would be of the utmost importance.

"Keep alert, they won't be stupid enough to come around the corner without some kind of support," Garath growled. He had given up on mind speak to save his magic, he had a feeling he was going to need every last bit of it soon.

As if Garath's warning was a trigger a large net

dropped from the top of the keep completely covering the white dragon. "We need that roof cleared, be careful of the archers," roared Garath, angry at himself for thinking two dimensional in their assault. Dragons usually attack from above, not humans.

Without hesitation, the blue dragon blasted the top of the keep with his lightning breath. Stones exploded off the ramparts. With a bound, he leaped onto the keep wall and started climbing. The blast didn't do much damage but kept the archers back long enough for him to reach the top. Climbing over the edge he found six men wrestling with another net. The blue dragon's burst had apparently tangled up their plans so to speak. The soldiers were unprepared for such a quick response and were easily dealt with.

Garath turned his attention to the white dragon. The netting was getting more tangled as the large creature struggled. "Hold still, let me find the end and get it pulled off of you." The white dragon was near panic but was able to hold still long enough for him to grasp the edge and yank it free.

Garath yelled up to the blue dragon "cover us from the roof, your lightning shoots farther than our breath weapons." Without waiting for a reply Garath and the white dragon raced down the back of the keep to where hopefully Dram's group was fighting. As they got close, the sounds of all-out battle were underway.

Dram's team had rounded the front corners of the castle and was heading towards the back when Andrinin let out a scream in mind speak.

Eggs, they have my eggs here! Pulling up she concentrated on where the sensed the strongest presence of her unborn eggs. Without a word, she flew over the castle wall. Hundreds of arrows greeted her as she tried to get to where she could feel her children.

"No!" roared Dram as he tried to keep his mate from entering the courtyard. It was too late. His love fell from the sky, falling inside the castle courtyard. Flame erupted from Dram's mouth as he flew over the wall. Anyone on the ramparts was burned alive as he swept through trying to reach his mate.

As he crested the parapet, Dram found out the error in his plan. The courtyard was filled with men, hundreds in fact. This was a trap with one plan in mind, to lure as many dragons here as possible and annihilate them. Dram had led them right into it.

Dram's team followed him over the wall using flame and lightning to clear the area around Andrinin. Rushing to his mate Dram clawed the lancers that were trying to finish her off. While the other dragons landed to keep the area clear, Dram moved next to his mate. Arrows bounced off his scales as the farther-reaching bowmen took shots from the front of the castle.

"They have the eggs here! My babies are here!" Blood came out of Andrinin's mouth as she coughed, trying to speak.

"Stay still, we will get you out of here." Dram lowered her head to the ground as the light faded from her eyes. "My children," was all she could whisper as her body slowly faded away in Drams hands. The graveyard was taking her now so that no human could use her body to make arcane relics.

The pelting of arrows brought Dram out of his trance. He could feel what Andrinin was telling him. Some of his eggs were here in the castle. Looking around Dram could see that only three dragons from his team were left. Two more had fallen to well placed or lucky arrow shots. *I am going inside the castle. Can you handle it out here?* Dram spoke to one in his group. Hearing an affirmative, he headed to a set of double doors of the keep itself.

Rearing up on his back legs, Dram leaped into the doors, shattering them in half. A hallway led into the keep just big enough for him to crawl down. He sensed his eggs were close. Working his way down the tunnel, he could not sense anyone in the castle. They must be all outside, he thought. The passageway opened up into a great hall, in the middle of the room was a large table with five dragon eggs in the center.

"So, you made it after all." The voice came from across the table on the other side of the eggs. Two high backed chairs sat facing the fire away from the table. Out of each stood a man, one in rich lavish robes and the other in full armor.

"Magi!" Dram spit out the word like acid. Now he understood how they got in without detection and was able to do so much damage. They had ways of not being detected, even by his race. They used the dragons own magic against them.

"Yes, and this is Lord Lombard, ruler in this region. You have raided his lands long enough dragon and now we are putting a stop to you and your kind." The two men were using the eggs as a shield. Dram could do nothing while his children were between them.

As Dram took a step closer, Lord Lombard pulled his sword and held it over one of the eggs. "No closer dragon or we finish what we started yesterday." Dram halted trying to figure out how he could get around the eggs to the men behind them. The magi kept talking but the words were lost on the dragon. He tried to think of some way out of this, to save his family, but he could only come up with one. Dram could only carry one egg. No matter what he did four of his children would die to save one. There was no way he could leave them in the hands of humans, especially Magi. Knowing that thinking would only slow the inevitable, he acted.

Rushing forward, he went straight for the one with the sword. As soon as he moved, the Lord of the castle brought down the weapon cleaving the egg in half. Before he could get a second stroke, Dram cleaved him in half with one mighty slash of his claw, his limp form slamming against the back wall near the Magi.

Pain exploded in Dram's side as an energy bolt burst from a staff the magi was holding. Again, some kind of energy shot out of the device and hit Dram, this time in the shoulder. The magi had underestimated Dram, for he could no longer feel much pain or care. Whipping his tail around, he smashed the robed man into the fireplace. The magi screamed as the burning wood scorched his skin and set him ablaze.

No longer interested in the man, Dram once again turned his attention to the eggs. Their life force was almost gone, the cold severely weakening them. Finding the strongest of the four remaining eggs, he gently picked it up in his mouth and moved it to the hallway leading outside.

Gently laying the egg down on the floor, he again turned to face the last of his children. *Forgive me!* He thought as he opened his mouth to let the burning fire consume the room. What was left of his children turned to ash from the dragon's flame. So intense was his rage that the very stone started to melt in the room. The fire started to spread to the other rooms as Dram gently picked up his last child and started to make his way down the hall.

Dram we are trying to hold the way open for you, but we are losing fast. The arrows are taking their toll. I'm not sure how long we can keep this up. Hearing Garath's voice helped Dram to focus on what needed to be done. *I am coming out; I will need cover to get sky born.* As Dram reached to broken doors that led outside, he could make out just how bad their losses were. Only four dragons remained, and they were using everything they had to keep the courtyard open in front of the doors. *Get going Dram we will keep them off you.* Dram raced through the doors and leaped skyward. Within two wing beats, he was over the wall and heading to the edge of the valley with the egg still held softly in his mouth. Looking back Dram made out the shapes of Garath and Lo'Lith as the only two following. *They are making sure we escape,* Garath told him. He knew they would not be able to escape themselves but were giving their lives for the rest of them.

The three remaining dragons landed on the hillside where they had first glimpsed Greytock. The battle still raged on inside the courtyard. The fire was climbing higher as the blazes set both by Dram and the other dragons spread out of control.

"Please take this back to the hatchery Lo'Lith, Garath and I have some unfinished business." Clearly shaken by the whole ordeal she could only nod. Picking the egg up from where Dram set in on the ground she hurried back to the hatchery to get the egg warm again.

Turning to Garath Dram said, "We let the fire burn a little more, the humans think we have fled. With the smoke, it should conceal our approach and allow us to finish what we started. No one will leave that place to tell stories about what happened, in the hatchery or in the castle." Garath could only nod in agreement, as they both sat on the valley ridge and watch the fires burn higher.

Dram and Garath landed on the ledge outside the hatchery. The confusion from the fires and smoke had made it easy for them to finish off everyone in the castle. No one would live to spread the word of killing so many dragons and their young.

The fires of the hatchery were burning bright as Dram came through the doors. Ash covered the sandy floor from where Lo'Lith had used her own fire to burn what was left of his children. A single egg sat in the middle of the room warmed by the braziers on the side. Tears fell from Drams cheek at the site. So much was lost now. Only this one thing still kept him alive, the needs of the last of his children.

"Thank you Lo'Lith, I will take it from here." Without a word, she left to the outer rooms as Dram lay on the sandy floor surrounding an egg that was still cold from its ordeal. Outside Dram could hear Garath singing a song to Saris, asking him to take care of the fallen and see to their place in the dragon's graveyard.

The nights and days passed for a full moon as Dram stayed by the egg never moving. Garath would bring him food though he ate little, his skin turning darker and darker as the days went on. The egg should have hatched many days ago, but Dram still held out hope. That is all he had, even though he could feel no life in it since returning to the hatchery. There was nothing else for him now, no purpose, and no reason for going on.

"Dram, its time to go. The Council has asked you to come and tell what happened at Greytock. There is no life-force in the egg anymore, I am sorry." Dram knew what Garath was saying was true, but he could not face it, not yet. How had he failed his family so badly? Rising from the sand, Dram turned and looked once more upon the last of his family. The tears no longer ran down his face, the anger all gone. Only a black emptiness in his heart that was colder than any winter he had ever known.

Garath moved outside while he waited for Dram to finish inside the hatchery. Stopping as he left the oval room, Dram turned and burned the room with hot acid from his mouth. The acid ate his stillborn child and melted the rest of the room beyond use. Toxic fumes burned his eyes as he turned and made his way to the ledge outside. The once golden dragon entered into the sun the deepest obsidian. The black dragon looked back at the entrance of the hatchery only for a brief instance.

Launching off the ledge, Dram turned and headed northeast to the where the dragon Council met. Garath followed closely behind.

Dram found himself again on the barren plain. This time there was no grey just the translucent shade of silver. The light was now gone but everything seemed to glow with a sort of radiance. Ahead of him sitting on the so-called grass was Saris.

"Welcome back my brother," said the platinum dragon. "Did you finally come to grips with yourself?"

"I think so, I miss my old life, but the hate is gone and the anger." Dram could not help but shake. He was tired, his mind was spinning. The dragon felt different, but he could not tell how. Only that he now remembered everything that happened those twenty years ago and not really sure how but could accept them.

"Then sleep, like you have not in years. You have finally forgiven yourself and your enemies. Most of all you remembered the love you had once. We will talk more later on. Sleep for now and your change will be complete." Dram did not know what Saris meant by the last comment but was too tired to care. Laying his head on his forelegs, he finally slept, as he had not since that day before Greytock. Dreams of Andrinin flying by his side over warm mountain peaks filled his mind. Gone was the guilt of still being alive. Only the joy, for he again remembered the love he had with his mate.

CHAPTER 13

The morning sun warmed Dram's face as he groggily awoke, still on the ledge before the twin dragon statues. The darkness of the cave between them seemed to envelop the new rays of light, making the tunnel seem darker than in the purest night. Something was different from the evening before, or at least what he thought was the night before. He had no idea how long he had been out.

As Dram lifted his head, he noticed something was not right with his color. His skin, that was obsidian before was now almost silver, more than that, it was slightly transparent, like quartz. Remembering his dream, Dram thought that Saris was similar in color. There was only one dragon in history that achieved that platinum color. He supposedly died creating the dragon's graveyard. Looking at the rest of his body, he found the same color ran the whole length. If he wasn't dreaming, somehow, he was now a platinum dragon, the epitome of his race. Brushing his delusions of grandeur aside Dram concentrated on his mission.

Dram looked above the cave to what remained of the large mountain above. The cliff wall rose several hundred feet climbing into the sky, looming ominously over the small ledge on which he now stood. There was no path leading up the mountain to the small outcropping of stone. It was as if it formed out of the very side of the granite mountainside itself. Below the shelf, several hundred feet of cliff fell to the glacier. There was no way humans could make it even close to the entrance of the graveyard, however, Dram knew there was more protection inside. The two statues that shocked him unconscious still stood before him looking harmless.

"So what surprises do I have awaiting me now?" Dram said to himself. If it was true that this place was built by Saris, it should not hurt him, he hoped. That wouldn't mean though that there wasn't more in store for him. With no sense in waiting, he walked into the darkness between the two statues using his inner site to guide his way as well as it could.

The tunnel ended not long after it began into a huge cavern. The ceiling was so high that he could not see it, even with his sight. In the center on a pedestal sat what looked like a dragon egg, but instead of the opaque shell of a normal egg, it was like a huge diamond. Curled around the pedestal at the base was another statue of a dragon, this one was more lifelike than the ones outside and easily 3 times bigger than Dram. The crystal-like egg sat at the same height, as Dram's head, easy enough to reach for a dragon. Still, he expected some kind of trial. Saris would not just let any dragon come in to take the most sacred of dragon relics, The Orb of Saris.

Trying not to touch the sleeping statue after his ordeal with the last ones, Dram took a closer look at the Orb. It just sat in a pocket at the top of the pedestal. Nothing seemed to lock it down or be protecting it that he could see with his inner sight. Bringing his magic to bare he tried to move the orb but to no avail. Trying one last thing Dram simply touched the Egg.

Power blasted out from the orb in all directions, passing through Dram without effect but shaking the whole cavern enough to make him lose his footing falling on the statue below him.

"Would you please get off my tail?" an annoyed voice said from beneath him. Dram jumped back off the statue as it rose to stand in well above him. Shaking off the dust of ages from his body, in front of Dram again stood Saris.

"Is this a dream again? Is there another test?" In his mind, Dram was ready for anything, except what the dragon in front of him said next.

214

"Are you a dragonette? Or maybe the runt of the litter? I have never seen a full-grown dragon so small." said the mammoth statue with a slight laugh.

Dram was too mentally drained to take offense. "This can't be real, I must still be in that nightmare."

"This is about as real as it gets Dram. You have set in motion events that we cannot turn away from now. We can only try to guide those events so that the future of our race is not completely lost. By the way, do you have any food? I am starving."

The change of topic completely sidetracked Dram. Shaking his head negatively was all he could muster. Finally gathering his wits around him, the only thing he could ask was "I thought you were dead."

"If I was dead would I be hungry? Come on boy, I know you are not that slow." The same irritating tone from the dream caused Dram to cringe. After all he had been through. To be scolded like an infant, even if he was an infant to someone as old as Saris.

"Its ok Dram, when you get as old as I am you will understand that taking things too seriously can be as bad as not serious enough. In time you will see, you have taken a big step towards enlightenment but there is still far for you to go." Saris nodded towards Dram's front leg, the color of which was the same as the dragon before him. Nevertheless, there was a difference, Saris's skin was opaque and Dram's was slightly transparent. The meaning of which was lost on Dram but not on the dragon in front of him.

"Dram you have seen the elation of intelligence and the despair of losing those you love. You have hated more than any dragon in history because you cared more than any in thousands of years. You will surpass me, in fact, you already have. However, you have a lot to learn, and a lot I need to teach you. Enlightenment does not mean knowledge, its understanding of how events interact in the universe. Every action no matter how small has one or more reactions. These may be equal to the action, greater or so small the relevance isn't known until later. At the moment, this is the vicious cycle our race is in. Do you understand what I am saying?"

With the hate gone, Dram could fully analyze the events of the past twenty or more years. "Yes, I know exactly what you mean. It took me so long to see it, never would have if you hadn't shown me."

"I was asleep so don't blame me for your delusions, I just nudged you in a direction and you took it from there. If I would have just shown you, we would not be here now discussing this." Saris's tone was off-handed, almost as if he was trying to get out of being blamed for a misdeed.

"What I mean is I understand the action-reaction statement you described. I thought the attack on my family was unprovoked, but it wasn't. Dragons were raiding the land under the old Dukes protection. He fought back with attacking my family. All he knew was a dragon was a dragon. In essence, he was actually a good man, fighting for his people, for their protection. I killed him for what he did, for revenge but in doing so I set forth events that led to his grandson taking up the cause. Now the new Duke is not just out to stop raiding on their livestock. He is out to destroy us all and he has a vast amount of resources to accomplish that. Something he has been putting together for twenty years, what you said of too small to notice ripple effect."

Saris only nodded in agreement as both were silent, mourning those that had pasted for needless causes. The dust of ages around them echoed the lives of dragons spent over millennia.

"I need to tell you a story, one you will not know from your genetic memory. Honestly, I may be the only one that knows of our history now. Thousands of years have passed since I first created this place, but every so often from those that come here, I get glimpses of what is happening in the world. It saddens me how far our race has fallen from the actions of a few."

"We are not of this world. We are refugees from a place where gods battled. Slaves in a sense although we thought we were allies to the old ones. While the battles raged, I found a way for those of us that knew the truth to escape to a new domain. Over one thousand of us, a small fraction of our race made it here to earth. We thought that we could start fresh, a world of our own. Soon we learned of a primitive animal that had evolved past all others on this planet, it was man. Still in their infancy, they could draw fire from the earth and forge crude weapons."

"We thought we were being benevolent taking them under our wing and teaching them the wonders of the world. We built great cities together, huge monuments to our achievements all over the world. Together we accomplished more than either of us could have done on our own. However, that was not enough for us, we came from slavery and now we wanted to be the masters. Some of us pretended to be gods, others created great empires leading the humans to war in both spiritual and greedy aspirations. The humans caught us pretending to be their gods and a war erupted."

217

"We were not all trying to make them slaves, but a few of us ruined it for all. The vast works we did together, huge pyramids to the south and across the sea. Our greatest achievement was a floating city that housed the pinnacle of all man and dragon kind. This is where the last battle of our war happened. We had taught the humans too much about how to use our life force, the battle was bloody. We won but at great cost, if truth be told I think we lost that battle in the end, the way our race is now."

Dram was in shock from the story he was told. All the legends he was told about the wonders of the human race were now inspired and destroyed by his race because of their own power lust.

"Dram I need you to understand. If the dragons and humans go to war again like you intend we will lose. Not only our race but also our heritage. We will put up a noble fight, be assured. But this is a fight we fought before, there is no winner. Our only chance is to survive long enough to find a place where we are the only beings of power. Our nature dictates it, more than that, our race needs it to rebuild. We have lost so much of ourselves just trying to live that we have forgotten who we are and what we can be."

Dram could fully understand the last statement that Saris had made. He was trying to rebuild his race with his mate Andrinin when everything went to darkness. Now he could see that the darkness wasn't about the war with the humans but in his own people. For thousands of years, the dragons took what they wanted because we could, not thinking that year's later suppression would rise up to bite them in the tail.

"So, what now? If we don't go to war, then we end up getting ripped apart one by one to this new threat." Dram was at a loss, although he could understand that the dragons had gotten themselves into this mess, he still had to find some way to save his people.

"What you call the Orb of Saris is still going to be your savior, but not the way you think. It has absorbed the life force from all dragons for the past three thousand years. Ever wonder why dragons are the only creatures on this planet with any magic? But that magi can channel magic to do great deeds for good and evil from any once living item?"

Dram had dwelled on this for years but to no solution. He had always thought they were the same thing, just that the humans didn't have a magic of their own. Shaking his head yes, Saris continued.

"There is magic, and then there is life force. I know you have been taught that these are the same, but they are completely different. Two paths of power, you can think of them, but in the end, it is power from your mind or power from your soul. I can tell you, your soul is ten times more powerful than your mind. This is what we taught to humans since their intelligence could not handle the mind form of magic. They learned quickly how to harness the power of the soul in objects living or dead. Lifeforce powers every being on this planet. It interacts, intertwines in ways that the oldest of us don't fully comprehend. However, one thing is for certain, it is an entity of great power and if properly channeled can do inordinate good or harm, far more than we dragons can do on our own. This is a power that you now possess and must learn to control with your new transformation."

"So why don't we use this against the humans? We taught them this power, can we not harness the dead for our own purposes? If I have this power now why can't I use it against them?"

Saris shook his head; a sad loss crossed his face remembering the past. "We did it once and we destroyed a city. We didn't stop there we used it again and we wiped out a whole nation. The retribution of the dragons had no end. We would have wiped the entire human civilization from this planet if I hadn't done what I did."

Saris paused as if a heavy burden was still weighing down on him. "I may have doomed our race Dram. I saw what we were doing to humans and to ourselves. I didn't create the dragon's graveyard to save us from humans. I did it to save us from ourselves. Once the humans were wiped out, the only adversary was each other. War had bent the minds of our race, making them forget the legacy of knowledge that was theirs."

"Now I ask you are you ready for what has to come next? The orb can hide our kin as humans. Not just as images but as actual men and women able to move freely within human society. We have to do this while I am gone, or I may not return to our race still being alive."

Dram was still reeling from the knowledge that Saris was imparting on him. The oldest dragon on the Council was only a little over one thousand years old. This was someone that was over ten thousand years old according to legend and had seen it all. What was he to someone like that?

"So instead of going to war, we should join man? Become like them?" even in his new enlightenment Dram almost spit the comment out.

"Can you think of a better way to survive? At least until I return with something better to help us with. Now take the orb and head out, I have a lot of work to do. I have set it to transform a dragon to human form when it is touched and the phrase "I will Submit" is spoken."

Dram knew the conversation was over. Although his enlightenment may be the same as Saris, there was still so much he needed to know. His knowledge was too limited to be of much use to the old dragon. Grabbing the egg-shaped crystal in his mouth, Dram followed Saris out of the cavern and onto the ledge outside. It wasn't even mid-day yet, the sun shining high in the morning sky.

"Take care Dram, when I find a haven for our people I will be back. Until then you are their protector, a tough job with what is coming." Nodding, Dram launched off the cliff, wings out catching the updrafts from the cold winds rising from below. Looking back, one last time, Saris was nowhere to be seen. Feeling somehow alone, he headed back to the Council wondering why the old dragon thought he was a dragonette.

Dram reached the cratered mountain that was home to the Council the next day. The shock was an understatement to the reaction that greeted him from the dragons he passed. His new color was starting to make a sensation. Heading straight for the Council, he brought the orb that he hoped would be the savior of his race. Within minutes of entering the chambers, word of his transformation had spread throughout the mountain. The silver dragons were quick to assemble to hear both of the orb and what was considered a myth, the platinum dragon.

Dram told the Council of his adventure and the discussion with Saris, from changing the plans of going war to one of hiding among the humans. If it weren't for his new color, the story he told would have been taken as an all-out lie. For hours they talked, discussing all the alternatives but in the end, they knew that Saris was right. War with humans would eventually bring their own end.

The Council recessed for a day allowing Dram some needed rest. The flight back was taxing for he used most of his magic to make the trip, leaving him drained. He went to find Garath, who he was sure was with Danielle. A short time later, he found them both in human form outside in the crater.

"So, the rumors are true, you are all shiny." Garath laughed as he gave his friend a hard time. The laugh was infectious for both Dram and Danielle.

Dram told them both about his trip and the Council meeting. Garath for once was speechless when told of Saris and their discussion. Danielle listened thoughtfully, almost wanting to interrupt with a question but waited for the end.

"Dram it might be better if you go to war. Do you understand the logistics involved in what you are suggesting? Not to mention clothing, food or money you can't just take several hundred dragons that look like humans and integrate them into society, especially when most of them wouldn't have the first clue of how a human behaves, especially around others." Danielle's words stung like a whip, Dram knew this was going to be tough on everyone, but in his rush to get back to the Council he never fully thought out all the small details that would be needed.

"Those are good points, we have four months to prepare before the gathering. This isn't something we want to do. It is our last hope. If we go to war, we all will die and lose any heritage that the dragons still hold."

Garath never one for a moody talk tried to lighten the situation "So who's going to be the first dragon to test this thing? I want to do it."

Dram and Danielle both looked like they were struck with lightning. Before any could say a word, Garath was making his case. "Look, besides yourself, who knows more about how to blend in with humans? Danielle, you said it yourself, we need to not only look human but also act human. We have four months before the gathering, at that time Danielle and I can find our people a home. I am guessing that Bowlsy fellow you mentioned might have some ideas. Thing is I can't do this as a dragon, two weeks was about all I could handle between lack of sleep and food, four months would be impossible for anyone. Not to mention the distance we would have to travel over open ground, even flying at night best I could do is about fifty miles a day, especially since our princess here doesn't like to travel lite."

Danielle, already used to Garath's humor, poked the dragon in the stomach. "Seems I am not the only one that travels heavy, least I can drop my luggage. I think all the easy meals up here has added a few pounds to you."

Garath, trying to suck in his gut replied. "It was from worrying about you, if this is how things are going to go around you then I am afraid I will never be thin again." The sincerity of his comment made them all laugh.

Dram hadn't thought of who would be the first one to be turned human. With everything that had happened within the last couple of weeks he was just trying to get the orb back to the Council and let them decide what to do with it. Seems his role in all this was far from over.

"I need to rest. I used all my powers for the return. I will think about what you said and suggest it to the Council. I hope you realize what you are getting yourself into." Dram still couldn't understand what his friend was intending, too tired to think about it, he headed off to one of the caves entering the crater.

Garath turned to Danielle as his friend left for some sleep. Tears ran down her cheeks from both joy and sorrow. Too bittersweet was the offer that Garath had put forth. "You can't do this for me, to lose all that is you for what?"

"I do this for my people, that you are here with me is the only thing that gives me the courage to even think of it. Imagine another dragon even Dram, trying to make it in human form without someone like you to guide them. They wouldn't get far, nor would they know where to go. Danielle, I really believe this is the best course, we can set up a way for the dragons to get to safety, where ever that is."

Garath's words did little to alleviate Danielle's concerns but she knew he was right. The dragons best chance rested in the relationship they had.

"How is your injury? Think you are about ready for a journey?"

Danielle flexed her shoulder, still feeling the tightness and some pain where the crossbow bolt had hit. "It's better, I should be able to ride a horse, but not sure how long."

"How about a dragon?" The young woman stood speechless as Garath transformed into his natural form.

Golden scales glistening off the setting sun as he towered over her.

"If I am to try out this orb and become locked in human form I would like to show you a little of the wonders about being one of my kind." As he spoke he lowered his shoulder and neck so that she could easily step up onto his back.

"What about a saddle or tack?"

"I'll protect you, and wouldn't you just love to put a leash on me," he said jokingly.

With a slight smile, Danielle stepped up on the dragon's forearm and using her good hand swung herself up onto his back, sitting just in front of his wings.

"Ready?"

"You bet!" The excitement ringing in her voice.

Without hesitation Garath launched into the sky, the power from his wings rippling the water as he flew out over the lake.

"Up for a bath?"

"You better not!" She yelled as she playfully slapped his shoulder. Banking, Garath turned to catch the warm currents rising from the hot springs. The air pushed them up to the rim of the crater, now able to view the peaks in the distance.

"It's breathtaking, I never knew I would see such views."

The sun was just starting to set over the western mountains sending halos of orange and blue across the horizon.

"Garath, how could your people ever give this up?" The golden dragon only sighed as he hovered above the highest crest allowing Danielle to survey the snowcapped peaks.

"Here in the mountains, so far away from the humans, it is going to be very hard to convince the others what is taking place. It is going to be a rough time for us all."

Danielle could feel the sadness come from Garath as he spoke. She then laid her head against the dragon's warm neck, feeling his steady breathing as he kept them both in flight.

Softly as if humming a tune to himself the dragon started to sing, first there were no words then as the song progress Danielle could make out a language. Although unclear to her ears the words made sense in her mind.

The approach of night
Sun falls from the sky
It touches the earth
Into the stars we fly
Our one great hope
The platinum dragon will try
To free us all
Existing was our only crime

A light through the darkness
Shows us the way
Escape from the shadows
For only death if we stay
Saris will lead us
Through the darkening night
To a new home
Our hopes now burn bright

Tears streamed down Danielle's cheeks as Garath finished the song. "That is so beautiful, I didn't know dragons sang songs." She spoke softly, laying the side of her face on the dragon's warm neck.

Garath was silent for a minute before he answered. "It's an ancient song, from a time when my people were more scholars than warriors. What we do now is to make sure that legacy will not die."

They floated in silence on the dragon's wings, letting the touch of being together be all the communication they needed.

"We better head back, it's getting cold fast." Although Garath was fine he was worried about Danielle's frail condition.

"I know but I don't want to stop, not ever."

"Alright, one more pass around the mountain. After that, it will be too dark to see."

The sun farthest peaks as Garath banked and headed back towards the cave entrances. The crisp mountain air waned as they descended into the crater itself. Softly landing on the rocky shore Garath said: "We are here."

Reluctantly Danielle let go of the dragon's neck and stepped shakily onto the ground. Garath transformed back into his human form, the glow lighting up the still rippling water.

No more words were spoken as Danielle leaned into Garath grabbing him around the waist. They both just stared into the heavens surrounded by the rim of the crater. The faint sparkles of stars started to litter the sky following the decline of their competition. Slowly the couple walked back to the alcove where they were staying.

The next morning the three of them were summoned to the Council hall. No one really slept, including the members of the Council themselves. The nine silver dragons, each perched on their own raised rock slabs, were ready to pronounce their decision.

"After our discussion last night Dram, the Council agrees to your proposal. You are right, there is a great risk on both sides of the issue of going to war or hiding in human form. I am told that our new friend Danielle is to thank for this eye-opening introspect."

Garath and Danielle stood confused at the comment made by the lead speaker. They could only conclude that Dram had talked to them after their talk outside in the crater.

"Garath, I am told that you want to volunteer to be the first one to test being turned human. Are you sure you are ready for such an undertaking?"

Garath still surprised by what was happening answered, "Yes I am."

"Danielle, you have been with us only a short time but after saving the life of one of our own at the risk of your own, and further knowing you from your stay here we consider you a friend. Do you believe what we plan to do has any chance of succeeding? Can we hide among your people until the day Saris returns with hope for a safer place?" The lead speaker placed the highest compliment a dragon could on Danielle by calling her friend.

"It will be hard, I have many contacts but so does my brother. If we can reach the north where we are told, "we both have friends" then maybe we can set something up to get your people safely there. All I can tell you is that Garath and I are your best bet for achieving this."

Danielle had no problem talking to the Council. Years of

court upbringing had conditioned her to speak in public, to be direct or evasive when needed. This was time for directness.

"Then it's settled, Garath please step up to the orb." The Orb of Saris had been placed in the middle of the Council chamber on a slender column. Garath moved up to stand in front of the relic not sure what to do.

"Touching the Orb and saying "I Will Submit" will begin the transformation. You will look like you do now but will be fully human with most of the weaknesses any human would have except your lifeforce will give you a few benefits like strength and stamina. You will also age differently than in dragon form, the orb can't change your life force, but it uses it to keep you in human form. It will tend to burn more rapidly, we don't know what that means for how long you could live. It can be anywhere between a human or a dragon."

Garath started to reach up to the orb then hesitated. Looking back at Danielle was all the resolve he needed as he once again looked at the egg-shaped crystal and placed his palm squarely on the middle. As he said the words he noticed the orb was strangely warm, like it was alive, pulsing under his hand. Slowly he removed his hand, it seemed nothing had happened. Turning to his friends, something felt different, he had bumps in places he didn't have before, like between his legs, making walking awkward.

Looking down he was completely naked. The orb had truly turned him into a human. Testing the new form, he walked to an open area of the chambers and tried to release his magic to his dragon form. Nothing happened. Most of his other powers were gone also.

"Strange, I feel like my wings have been clipped. I am not sure how most of our kin are going to take this. I seem to be completely human, even down to some basic parts" Garath checked his body trying to see what was new to his old form. Pulling a dagger out he made a small cut in his forearm. Red blood started to flow out of the incision and down onto his hand.

"It seems its complete, any side effects you can tell?" Garath shook his head no, still wondering what inner changes he went through. "Then we will meet in a week's time, test your new body thoroughly, we need to know if this is going to be something all our kin can undertake. Danielle, I know we don't have to ask this, but can you look after him and teach him the not so pleasant parts of being human that he might not already know? I understand if this might not be comfortable for you." The lead speaker was trying to be as compassionate as possible, but time was of the essence.

"I will try to be as gentle as possible, probably starting with how to eat with his mouth closed and move on from there." Danielle was starting to have a little too much fun with this now. Garath's laid-back attitude was going to suddenly change with this new challenge and she was going to delight in being there when it did.

Danielle could have sworn the speaker smiled at her remark as he nodded to their group. "The gathering is in four months, at that time we decide if we go to war or hide in human form. Saris guide us all." Turning he crawled out of the chambers with the other Council members.

Garath, not to be outdone by Danielle's remark. "So just what can you teach me? I hear the human mating rituals can be, ah quite lengthy." Danielle turned beet red at his remark as she tried to redirect the comment.

"Well, you are going to have to get rid of that dragon's breath of yours before you are ever going to find out." Without waiting for a reply Danielle walked out of the room, Dram laughed hard for the first time in years stunning his friend even more than Danielle's comment.

"You have your hands full there my friend, but I must say, it's worth holding on to." Garath only grinned at the dragon next to him.

"Welcome back my friend, and yes she is but I wouldn't trade any of it for the world. Just don't tell her that, she already has me wrapped around her finger. Is this what it was like for you?"

Dram paused a moment thinking of his love Andrinin. "Yes and no, we didn't have the weight of the world on our shoulders. We had time to fully explore our connection but until the end, we were never really tested. You and Danielle have been through the dragon's breath and yet in that, you have found the capacity to transcend race, sacrifice and losing your own power as a dragon. Its amazing to me."

"Well you know she is kind of cute, for a human that is." Garath, always ready to make a serious conversation into a joke, slapped his big friend on the shoulder as they walked out of the chambers after Danielle.

CHAPTER 14

Garath advanced on Dram bringing his shield to bare. A feint to the head with his sword caused his opponent to block, the gold dragon used the opening to bash his foe with the shield. Dram was ready for the attack and spun left around the shield and brought his sword up to Garath's unprotected throat.

"Better, but you overextended again, leaving yourself open. Don't fully commit unless you know your opponent can't escape."

Garath wiped the sweat from his eyes, being transformed by the orb was completely different than using his magic. He still had more strength and endurance than a human but was still nothing compared to a dragon. "I am still not getting it. How do you know for sure?"

Dram thought for a second before answering, Bowlsy was a great teacher and the dragon learned quickly, but that didn't mean he could as easily teach someone else to fight in human form. "From my experience, that is why you test your opponent's skill, don't go for the kill right at the start or it could be you. Once you wear him down, you should see your opening."

"Well I am definitely worn down, think its time to eat." Danielle laughed at Garath's remark from where she watched, sitting on a large rock next to the lake. Getting up she came over to the dragons, "Dram, sorry but I don't think you are training Garath correctly." Both of them looked confused at her comment. Hastily she continued to clarify, "I didn't say bad but I think Garath needs a little different style than yourself."

"So, we have a little sword instructor in our midst." Garath joked.

"Actually, I have more sword and hand to hand training that both of you put together." Danielle was getting tired of the defenseless girl identity both of them seem to put her in. She stood with one hand on her hip and the other stretched out, waiting for Dram to hand her his sword.

The former black dragon chuckled at the banter and handed over his sword. "I admit, I am not an expert by any means, especially in teaching a human how to fight."

Danielle grabbed the sword, then with a quick turn, smacked Garath on the arm with the flat of the blade, similar to what Captain Norjor did. "That's for doubting me!" Dram nearly doubled over in laughter at the stunned look on the dragon's face, it was as if she had just run him through with the sword.

"Garath, Are you ok? Are you going to listen?" Danielle said with the biggest smile on her face. The dragon just shook his head and gave in, what else could he do?

"Dram, Bowlsy taught you how to fight a good opponent, most likely in single combat. It takes years to learn to be that good, even with the best teachers. It was probably only your dragon abilities that allowed you to even fight at that level."

Dram was a little put off by the comment, then quickly realized she was just stating a fact. "That's true, I never would have been able to fight him without my heritage, no matter how good a trainer Bowlsy was. Even then, every time I thought I was catching up to him he would raise it to a whole new level. I am not even sure how good the man really was."

Garath shockingly kept quiet through the conversation, there was nothing he could say that wouldn't make him look more foolish than he already was.

Danielle continued, "Garath doesn't have most of his dragon abilities now and we don't have time for the years of training, maybe decades." She winked at Garath, enjoying herself a little too much. A smile crossed his lips as he still stayed quiet.

"My mother died with I was very young. My father, not knowing how to bring up a girl, raised me like my brother. Of course, he liked me best." She said the last with a bittersweet tone. Too much had happened too fast, she hadn't even begun to start processing it all. Pushing it aside she refocused. "Because of my size and the fact that I would never become a soldier, my father had me trained for a situation I would likely need it, being attacked by a group of untrained men. That may sound strange since I usually had guards to protect me, but even a small group can overcome a couple soldiers at a marketplace, an inn or like you witnessed, on a country road."

Now Garath spoke up, "So you didn't really need us after all, I could have gone hunting instead." The dragon's grin was infectious.

Mirroring his smile, she replied. "I wasn't exactly sitting on my cushions in the coach, I killed three of them before you got there. I would have been outside fighting with the soldiers but that would have been more of a distraction. They would have been trying to protect me than concentrating on the battle." Both dragons were more and more impressed with this woman at every turn.

Dram watched as Danielle went through several moves with Garath, quick strikes designed for opponents without much skill. What she said made a lot of sense to the dragon. They wouldn't be fighting soldiers, more like bandits, drunks and whoever else that thought they could take that wasn't theirs. Garath would learn quickly.

"You look like you are in good hands, Garath. I need to return to the Council, there is still a lot of planning to do." Garath tried to reply but Danielle launched a series of sword and hand attacks forcing his attention. Dram felt a warmness inside for those two. "Don't let up on him

Danny, he's getting soft hanging out up here." Dram turned and heading into the large cave mouth.

"OK, ok! I give, I can barely lift my arms now." They both laughed, each covered in sweat from their workout. Garath stripped naked and jumped into the lake, the hot springs keeping the lake from being too cold.

"One of the things I am going to have to teach you about humans is you can't just go running around naked in mixed company," Danielle said as she chided the dragon.

Garath was now swimming a few yards offshore, getting used to the sensation in human form. With a mischievous grin, he said, "Care to join me?"

With an exhausted sigh, she said, "Why not?"

Danielle laid in Garath's arms, the fur pallet they shared was itchy but warm as the night air turned cold. Strange sensations filled the dragon in his new form that he didn't feel before when she was near him. It was like the tension before a mating flight or battle mixed with a protectiveness that he had never felt for any other being, besides Danielle. He was excited and confused, wanting to act but too scared to move for the moment might stop.

The woman in his arms sensing his excitement reached up and gently kissed him. The touch was electrifying. Still, Garath only mirrored what Danielle started first. It was like the hunt. If you move two quick your prey will bolt. Unlike hunting, you hoped your target wanted to be caught, if only you don't mess it up.

Without knowing how Danielle was laying on his chest, her heart beat just as fast as his. Now another fear crept inside the dragon, he really didn't know what to do. For all his bravado and flirting with a human woman, he had never really gotten that far. It was just a little harmless fun. Now he was with someone he really cared about and the fear of not impressing her was making things worse to the point he was no longer, well longer so to speak.

Danielle stopped kissing Garath as wet tears fell from her cheeks landing on the dragon's face. Worried he had gone too far he started to panic, "I'm Sorry Danny, are you ok?"

"Yes, no, maybe, I don't know." Garath held completely still waiting for her to continue. "With everything that has happened, I just wanted this to be perfect, but I can tell you are just not into it and I feel like a fool." He could feel soft sobs on his chest as tears came to his own eyes, his heart nearly crushed by the pain of it. The dragon realized he just hurt the one he cared for the most, all he could do was to be completely open with her. He stroked the back of her hair, trying to think of what he could say to fix this. He gently lifted her head up to face his own. Wiping the tears off her cheeks with his thumbs.

"No Danny, I am so into IT and you, that I am scared stiff, or not, depending on how you look at it. I was afraid one wrong move would drive you away, then even worse I was afraid I wouldn't know what I was doing." Garath was having trouble getting the words out. His pride would not allow him to be so vulnerable except for his caring for the woman. He would do anything to make those tears go away.

Danielle started to giggle, then quickly turned into a laugh. Garath wasn't sure how to take this. Was she now laughing at him because he was weak?

"So, the big strong dragon is afraid of a little girl?" Garath got caught up in the laughter as he realized the absurdity of the situation. Again, he underestimated her strength, if he went too far she would definitely let him know, not run away like a frightened prey.

"Well, you were quite intimidating earlier when you were throwing me on the ground at training. I was too stupid to realize you wanted to start things then." Garath back to himself couldn't help the remark.

"Oh!" Danielle yelled, hitting him on the chest. "Well maybe if you could have stayed on your feet more, this could have started earlier. I had to wait for you to recover." They both burst into a fit of giggles that neither could stop.

This time it was Garath who started passionately kissing Danielle. They were clumsy at first, but the fear and tension were gone for both of them, only excitement and caring were left. The rest they figured out together.

Garath laid awake feeling the warm body of Danielle nestled on his shoulder. He could feel her warm breath caressing on his bare chest. Something new and amazing had just happened but he couldn't quite put his talon on it, it was something very different beyond the budding relationship. Then he realized what it was.

He was the prey and Danielle was the hunter, now he was definitely caught. Smiling down at the tangles of red hair, he thought to himself. There are far worse things than being caught, but he would never say it that way to her though.

Dram banked as he slowly descended towards the open clearing below. His two riders huddled together in furs to protect against the chill mountain winds. For the last week, Garath had trained, not only in fighting but human culture. He was a great student even without his dragon strength. Now the three of them would depart, all with their own missions.

Landing on the soft ground the platinum dragon searched the woods with his inner site to make sure no one was watching. Their decent went undetected as far as he could tell. Searching the trees there was not a human in sight.

Garath and Danielle dismounted with their supplies. "So where are you headed from here Dram? Back to the Council?"

"No, I have to find out what this new threat is up to and when. My guess is we only have until spring until they will show us. We need to know what it is and be ready."

"I have some contacts at my uncle's estates, they will not be happy after they find out what my brother has done. Garath and I will head there first then work our way north and see if we can't contact Bowlsy. We are going to need a lot of help in the future, hopefully, we can find it."

The platinum dragon looked down at his human companions. Words would not tell them what he felt. "Be safe you two. Danielle, would you make sure he doesn't get into trouble?"

Shrugging with a grin, she said, "I am not a miracle worker."

With that, Dram launched himself into the air, taking one last glimpse at his friends he headed east, becoming fully invisible with his newfound powers.

Danielle and Garath hoisted their packs and headed through the trees to a road that would lead them north and hopefully to new friends.

Norjor rode through the main gate of the northern keep. The men had been busy the last two weeks while he had been at the capital. The once rustic fort had been turned into the most modern of training grounds. Weapon racks lined several of the training areas while the whole compound was busy building everything from new structures to weapons of war. He could make out several engineers walking among the working mercenaries correcting their construction techniques.

The Captain drew his horse up in front of the steps leading up to the main doors of the keep. He paused as he considered only half a month before, the attack from the dragons had taken here, kidnapping his ward, someone he has protected most of her life.

"Sir, I can take your horse if you would like. Commander Shurlok should be in the war room." Shaken out of his introspect Norjor nodded to the guard, he had forgotten he still wore the tabard of the Captain of the Guard. Dismounting he handed the man the reins and grabbed several pouches out of his saddlebags.

"Please make sure my belongings get to where ever I am being billeted. I need to see Shurlok right away." The guard led his horse away as he started up the steps to the large double doors. "War room, hmm."

Moving through the doors Norjor paused to let his eyes adjust to the dim light. The hallway ahead opened up into a large common area but few torches lighted the room. Once in the center of the room, he could make out a faint light coming from an open doorway down one of the side hallways. With no other obvious option, the captain headed to the room. As soon as he entered one of the men stood up from a table filled with maps and papers to greet him.

"Captain Norjor, welcome. What news from the capital?" Shurlok slapped his hands together in anticipation as the captain handed over one of the satchels with letters from the Duke and his court.

"The coronation was the day before I left, kind of a somber ceremony with all that has happened of late," Said Norjor.

"I fully understand, and you will get your payback, we all will on those dragons. Come with me I want to show you something." Shurlok led the captain back out the front of the keep and out into the dirt courtyard.

"We just had a shipment of new weapons and armor arrive yesterday and the men are busy building the special training equipment we will need to do our next offensive. That is not what I wanted to show you." Norjor followed as Shurlok lead him into a large outbuilding set up in the corner of the marshaling yard. Inside a sickeningly sweet smell filled the air. Equipment similar to making spirits filled the room, while men and women in cloth masks worked at several tables.

"This is the key to what will be our revenge. The dragon's bane is processed, distilled and concentrated for greater effect. It allows it to be transported much easier. Our Magi are also working on new armor that will protect us from their magic. Once the men are trained we will take this war to the dragons themselves. When we are done there will be nothing left of their kind" Norjor could only stare amazed, a new form of warfare was being used now. An end, one way or another, would be soon.

Made in the USA
Lexington, KY
25 November 2019